Ta.X.I. to Angola

by

Jason Blacker

PUBLISHED BY:
Lemon Tree Publishing
Copyright © 2013
Jason Blacker

Visit www.JasonBlacker.com on the web to stay up to date

This is a work of fiction. All characters, names, places and events are the product of the author's imagination or used fictitiously.

Editing: Dragonfly Editing

ISBN: 9781927623244

Table of Contents

February 3, 2012 9:09 a.m.
Geneva, Switzerland

Lake Geneva is a gaping sad maw in the middle of Europe. It's a constant mouth of sadness. And on the far west end lay Geneva, the second largest city in Switzerland. Right on the edge, overlooking the Petit Lac, is a non-descript off white building. It is neither modern, nor old and decaying. It fits in well within its surroundings.

You've probably walked past it hundreds of time, not thinking much of it. And that is how it should be. In fact, many of you might have entered it to visit some of the shops there. I won't tell you which shops are in there, because I can't tell you which building in Geneva this is.

If I did, I'd have to kill you, as they say. Really. But in any event, if you're astute, you might have looked outside the building and counted six floors. And inside there is an elevator that goes to the sixth floor. But the sixth floor is not the top of this building. There is a seventh floor, and this is what concerns us.

Colonel Kade King is walking down the street wearing blue jeans a t-shirt and a black winter parka. His hair is short, in a buzz cut. In fact if you looked at him you might think he's ex-military, and he is.

Kade King came from the US Army Special Forces. You might know them as the Green Berets. It's not important where he's from. Some of you might think the Seals or the Rangers are more bad-ass, or even MARSOC, the US Marine Corps Forces Special Operations Command.

And you might be right. But we're not talking about a unit; we're talking about single men. And Kade King is a unique warrior, nay, a unique man, and that is why he has been chosen.

Kade walks into this seven-story building. In one of the shops he greets the manager behind the counter, who is an operative. The manager nods at him and smiles.

"I have some early bird specials if you're interested?" he asks.

"Tell me about the Sparrow's Dawn," says Kade.

"Yes, certainly, right this way," says the manager.

Kade follows him into the back through a biometric only accessible steel door. At the end of this room, which is set up like a storage area, the manager goes through another round of biometric identification. A drop of his blood is analyzed, his retina is scanned, his palm is scanned and an identification card is swiped as well. Added to this, he orally gives his daily password.

"Magic White Daytona Moon," he says.

A big portion of the door which has shelves and products attached swings open. Kade walks in alone. He has entered a lift. The manager nods and walks back out, only after the door has closed on Kade.

Kade is required to identify himself the same way the manager did. His blood is analyzed to verify his DNA. His retina is scanned as is his palm print. He swipes his identification card and offers up his one time password.

"Harry Hurry Tea Kettle," says Kade.

The elevator comes to life and starts travelling upwards. It is taking him to the seventh floor.

The seventh floor is where ANA is. ANA is the simple acronym for All Nations Alliance. It is exactly as it sounds. However, it is a non-political, private organization secretly funded through the United Nations. Their mandate is best described by their motto: Hominum Sunt Spem Ultimam or "Humanity's Last Hope." Some of the men call it the Hulahoop, coming from the first two letters of the first two words of the English version and bastardizing the last word.

They seek to bring long-term peace to the global arena, by any means necessary. The only reason Kade is here, is because he was invited. But more importantly, it means that he and his team are going to be going on a trip somewhere. Likely, somewhere exotic.

The elevator comes to a stop and the door opens again. Kade steps out into a large open reception area. Natural sunlight comes in through the ceiling, which is made of a high tech material that, when seen from the air, mimics a standard roof. Nobody can see in.

A very attractive woman with dark hair is sitting behind a desk. She looks up from her computer and smiles at him.

"Colonel," she says.

"Ms. Penny Whistle," he replies, smiling at her.

Our man Kade is in terrific shape. Although forty-three years old, he could easily pass for his thirties. He is muscular with the sinewy muscles of years of calisthenics, combat and physical exertion. Though he is handsome, he carries a three-inch scar down his left cheek at a forty-five degree angle to the horizontal.

Penny stands up from behind her desk. She is dressed in a tight fitting blue blouse and darker blue dress that hugs her legs just above the knees. Kade can't decide if the dress or the blouse is tighter. He admires them both.

"Mr. Drive is ready for you," she says.

"And you?" asks Kade, "Will you ever be ready for me?"

Penny looks at him with a mischievous grin and raises her right eyebrow. Kade feels his guts melt like butter.

"Maybe," she says, "when you ask with flowers."

Penny turns around and opens up a big wooden door. Kade smiles after her and walks into the office of Mr. Clive Drive. Clive is an older man in his early seventies. He's tall. Really tall. The file on him gives him a height of six feet seven. And he's a skeleton in it, with thinning white hair that he combs backwards. He always wears a black suit making him look much like a mortician.

The office is large and Clive is sitting at the head of an oval table. He gets up to come around and greet Kade. They shake hands.

"Good of you to come," says Clive.

"Happy to be here," says Kade, only half-jokingly.

"Come, sit down," says Clive as he ushers Kade over to a seat at the table.

Clive nods at Penny and she exits the room, giving Kade a warm smile. This is the main reason he likes coming here to ANA's headquarters. So he can see Penny Whistle.

Now I hear some of you snickering in the back. Don't. These are obviously not their real names. Like I said, if I told you their real names, I'd have to kill you. But these are the names they use and these are the names you'll see on their papers, like passports and such.

"We have a chap we'd like you to pick up," says Clive as if he were casually offering Kade a cab fare.

Kade nods.

"Tell me all about this chap or yours, then," he says.

Clive smiles and unbuttons his suit. He taps onto a computer screen located at his end of the desk and a hologram appears from the center of the desk. The lights in the room are automatically adjusted and dimmed.

Some video footage of a black man in army fatigues is shown. He is surrounded by a flock of lieutenants. The video footage ends and several photographic images are shown in the hologram. There is additional information such as the man's name, height, weight, and then a litany of charges that have been brought against him.

"This is Bernardo Bembe," says Clive, waving his hand casually towards the holographic image. "He is the leader of the Angolan People's Liberation Enforcement, or APLE for short."

"Apple, hey," says Kade. "That's cute."

Clive smiles.

"Yes, APLE for short. As you can imagine from their name, they enforce the liberation of the Angolan people. Or at least, that is what they are trying to do," continues Clive.

Kade nods. Bernardo Bembe is a stout, well fed, Angolan of average height. His face is mean and the best way that Kade can think of to describe him is that he has dead eyes. He looks like a spoiled child who has grown up to be a miserable son-of-a-bitch.

"Not since the Rwandan Genocide of '94 has there been this much bloodshed in Africa. According to reliable accounts on the ground, there have been over 5,000 disappearances of Angolans that we suspect are attributable to Bernardo Bembe."

"And I'm sure his mother still loves him," says Kade.

"His mother is dead," says Clive, "Bembe killed her. In fact he killed his whole family. His mother, younger sister and her son and his younger brother. His father died when he was a boy."

Kade nodded and looked at the image of Bernardo Bembe. It was his pleasure to bring men like him to justice.

"So you want us to bring him in alive?" asked Kade.

Clive nodded and sighed.

"I personally don't care if you bring him in alive or dead, though ANA's preference is that you bring him in alive to be tried for war crimes," says Clive. "This is why we have chosen you guys at Ta.X.I. 3 for the job. You're the best."

TaXI is another acronym, standing for Tactical eXtreme Insurgency. ANA is comprised of thirteen TaXI units of four men each. TaXI 3 was the first one created. Don't ask me why they were numbered 3 being the first, that's a long story.

Maybe I'll tell you about it sometime. In any event, three years ago when ANA was formed and the first TaXI unit was created there were over 10,000 Special Forces soldiers and militia who applied for the spots available. You do the math, but these are the elite of the elite. Four men to a TaXI unit and only 13 units, these guys are the best of the best. Sorry, but no ladies have been successful.

"You'll have all the support you need, as usual," said Clive. "The first part of your training will be languages. You'll need to have a working knowledge of Portuguese. Then, we'll brief you on tactics and terrain. Then, you'll be going in."

Clive leaned in towards Kade, resting on his elbows.

"Listen," he said, "time is of the essence. We want this chap back here in Geneva no later than Mother's Day, May 13."

Kade smiled at that.

"Cute," he said, "I think my mother would be proud."

February 6, 2012 8:08 a.m.

Somewhere in Maryland, USA

Colonel Kade King was going through his gear. He was kneeling down on the hard cement floor. He was wearing khaki cargo pants and a khaki undershirt. Over top he had on a leather bomber jacket.

This was a secure, converted, old airplane hangar owned by the CIA. Kade King and his team were here to learn Portuguese.

The large, metal, articulate door was closed. It was cold in Maryland. The lights were attached high up, near the ceiling. The 100 watt bulbs barely washed the hangar in enough light for Kade to see what he had in his pack.

Major Bain Blade walked in through a side door.

"Colonel," he said.

Kade looked up and smile broadly.

"Major Bain," he said. "It's been too long."

"Or not long enough," answered Bain.

They hugged each other, slapping each other on the back. Bain Blade had trained for several years with the British SAS. He was six feet three inches in stocking feet and built in a wiry muscular frame. He was South Asian and his British accent sometimes took people by surprise.

His nose had been broken one too many times, but he was ruggedly handsome with thick black hair and brown skin. He had recently celebrated his fortieth birthday, though that wasn't something he boasted about.

"It's only been three months since our last recce," said Bain. "You've kept yourself well, King."

His face was cut with a mischievous grin. Kade slapped him on the side of the shoulder.

"What can I say," said Kade, "I'm genetically gifted. I see your nose is still as straight as an arrow, Blade."

Kade winked at him. Bain rubbed his nose carefully.

"No matter," said Bain, "the girls like it."

Kade knelt back down and nodded his head.

"Yeah, I'm sure they do," he said.

"The others are in there," said Kade, cocking his head towards a door at the far end of the hangar, which held a large office area. "I'll be right along."

Bain slapped Kade on the shoulder as he walked on by and headed into the room. Seated around a large table were the other two members of TaXI 3. His compadres, and dear friends. Everyone was dressed in army fatigues. Major Sun Salt was in an army green t-shirt. Major Taye Tank had his jacket tightly wrapped around his thick, muscled torso. He looked up and grinned at Bain as Bain stood in the doorway for a moment. Taye's one gold tooth glinted, catching the bright light.

"Major Bain Blade," said Taye, standing up and laughing deeply, "I never would have thought it."

"Bullshitter," said Blade as he made his way around to give Tank a hug.

Tank was of average height, but weighed more than Blade's six foot three frame. He didn't get the name Tank by accident. He was a black South African, one of the very few to have reached the rank of Major in the South African Special Forces Brigade or Recces. He kept his head cleanly shaved and his dark chestnut complexion was darker than Blade's.

Underneath each eye he had an inch long horizontal scar. It was a right of passage, a coming of age he endured when he was thirteen as part of the Zulu culture. At least, that's what he tells people and they believe him. Truth is, he was captured once and branded by his torturers with a hot poker underneath each eye. He was a young thirty seven.

Blade let go of Tank and Tank went to sit back down.

"Damn it's cold in this place," said Tank.

Sun Salt rolled his eyes at Tank in a playful gesture. He got up and shook Blade's hand and gave him a courteous hug. Salt wasn't one for much physical contact unless it was fighting. Close combat was one of his specialties. He was of Chinese South American descent, but spent most of his youth and adulthood in Russia. He was, and still is, the only Chinese man to have been accepted into Spetsnaz and also the only Chinese man to reach rank of Major in the Russian Army. He was quiet, shorter than average at five feet six, wiry, handsome with jet black hair.

Sun Salt was also the oldest of the four at forty-five, but he looked to be the youngest.

He exuded a cool confidence and he was an impeccably efficient killing machine.

"My brother from another mother," said Blade.

They drew apart and looked each other.

"You think?" asked Salt, looking up at the tall, large frame of Blade's. He winked at Blade and turned around. That's when Blade slapped him on the back.

"It's okay, my brother, I've got your back," Blade said.

Tank laughed. Salt looked back and brought his foot up barely an inch from Blade's throat. Fast as lightning.

"Good one," said Salt.

Blade grinned at him.

"You know, got your back, I slapped your back," Blade said as he chuckled and pushed Salt's foot away.

"Dude, did you cut the cheese," said Blade waving his hand in front of his nose. "Them feet are stinky."

"Put a sock in it," said Salt smiling.

"Okay, children," said King walking in behind Blade and around to the head of the table. There was another man with him. He was wearing a black suit, his hair was short. He was obviously military.

"This is Captain Mike Pollard, and he's going to be our language teacher. Mike, to you," said King looking over at Captain Pollard.

King took a seat around the table as did Blade and Salt.

"Thanks, Colonel. Gentleman, as the Colonel said, I'm Captain Mike Pollard of language services for the CIA as well as FBI and NSA. Over the next sixty days we're going to get you up to speed on your Portuguese. And if you pay enough attention you might even make some inroads with Spanish Senoritas."

Mike put down the manila folder he was carrying. Then he opened it and took our four sheets of paper and handed them around.

"This is your curriculum for the next sixty days. As you can see, starting next week we're gonna have you guys immersed with local Portuguese speakers," said Pollard.

He looked around the room.

"Any questions?" he asked.

"What do you mean by up to speed?" asked Tank.

"I mean that after these sixty days you'll have near native fluency. I'd wager that you'll be able to wine and dine the finest Portuguese Senhoras."

Tank laughed loudly and deeply, like a metal chain dragged over a pebbly road.

"I think I like this guy already," he said.

TA.X.I. TO ANGOLA

May 7, 2012 01:01 a.m.

Somewhere over Cameroon

King undid his lap belt in ANA's Gulfstream V. The two pilots were ex-air force, though King hadn't known them. That wasn't unusual; he didn't know a lot of ANA's employees. They were cruising at an altitude of just under 50 thousand feet to avoid as much detection as possible and to cut down on any noise that might be heard on the ground. The G-V was cruising along at around 900 km/h.

King got up and walked towards the bathroom in the front between the door and the cockpit. Outside, through the porthole windows, the night was black, dotted with white stars as if someone and pricked holes in night's blanket.

Blade and Salt, opposite each other, were fast asleep, their chairs almost horizontal.

Tank was across from King reading a double issue of the April/May Asimov's Science Fiction. He was smiling to himself and didn't even look up as King passed.

King noticed the strange but well executed art of the cover included a fly. There would likely be a ton of flies where they were heading. King turned on the light and closed the lavatory door behind him. The noise of the jet engines was muted by the loud fan.

It was roughly a six and a half hour trip from Geneva to Kinshasa in the Democratic Republic of Congo. Being over Cameroon meant they had about an hour and a half left. Their ETA was in fact for 2:30 a.m.

King yawned and steadied himself against the wall of the lavatory. The ride had gotten bumpy and they seemed to be descending. "Perhaps we're getting in early," thought King.

He finished up in the lavatory and came back out. Blade and Salt were still sleeping like babies. Tank had finished with his magazine and had it on his lap. The fly on the cover was staring King down as he walked by.

Tank grabbed his elbow.

"Seems like we're descending," Tank said in a hushed tone.

King nodded.

"Maybe they've made up good time with a tailwind," he said.

Tank stared at him. King bent down on his haunches.

"I dunno, Colonel," said Tank. "I just don't have a good feeling about this."

King shrugged.

"It's not a big deal. We're on a scheduled six and a half hour flight. That's just under 400 minutes. Making up fifteen percent of that time with a good tailwind seems very doable."

King yawned. Tank slowly shook his head.

"I dunno King, doesn't seem right to me," Tank said. "Why haven't the pilots said anything, then?"

King looked down towards the back of the plane. Their gear was secured and lined up on both sides of the aisle where the other four seats would have been.

"You packed our parachutes, Tank?" asked King.

Tank nodded.

"I sure did," he said.

"Then we have nothing to worry about," said King.

"All right then, if you say so, Colonel," said Tank, picking up his magazine and opening it somewhere in the back.

King went back to his seat. He wouldn't mind getting a few minutes shut eye before they landed, but if they were getting in early, that didn't seem likely. He closed his eyes anyway and yawned. He was tired and it had been a long day full of briefings for the whole TaXI crew.

But what Tank had said was gnawing at him. Plus, it seemed they were descending more rapidly. It had been a few minutes and King figured they'd probably descended at least twenty thousand feet, if not much more.

King opened his eyes and looked at Tank. Tank wasn't wearing his lap belt. He had put the magazine on the small wooden table between them.

"I think I might go check it out," said King. "Just in case there's something wrong with the pilots. Maybe one of them's had a heart attack."

Tank nodded.

"And again I say, then why haven't they said anything?" he said.

"Stop being such a nervous Nelly," said King with a smirk.

He looked over at Blade and Salt. Still sound asleep. His guys had learned to sleep practically anywhere. Hell, one time they'd had to sleep in a ditch while a tornado rushed by. However, when things weren't right, the soldier's mind would wake you even from the deepest sleep. "Maybe they don't seem concerned by the descent," thought King.

He got up and walked past the toilet towards the cabin. He tried the door. It was locked. That was unusual, it shouldn't have been locked. King knocked on the door. There was no reply for a few seconds. He was just about to knock again when there was an answer.

"Just a minute," said one of the pilots through the door.

"Is everything okay?" asked King. "I've noticed we're descending quite fast."

"Everything's fine, Colonel," said the same pilot.

"We're descending to avoid some upper atmospheric turbulence. We didn't want to disturb you with an announcement. We thought you guys might be sleeping."

"Okay, thanks," said King.

He turned around and walked back to his seat. He was tired. He was definitely going to get some sleep for the last hour or so of this leg. Tank was off fiddling with one of the bags at the back. King watched him for a while.

Tank came back and sat across form King. He cocked his head upwards.

"No biggie," said King, "they're just trying to avoid some turbulence in the upper atmosphere."

Tank shrugged.

"Fair enough," he said.

Tank adjusted the watch on his wrist. It had an altimeter setting, which he looked at.

"You know we've just crossed under fifteen thousand feet," Tank said to King.

"Great," said King yawning and closing his eyes, "let me know when we get below one thousand feet and then I'll get worried."

Tank didn't say anything. The speed of descent was slowing. Everyone but him was asleep. He thought he'd try and catch some shut eye too.

It didn't last long. Perhaps a minute or two later he heard the cabin door open. Tank opened his eyes. The pilots were exiting the cockpit. That didn't seem right. Then he saw the pistol in each of their hands pointing down the hallway towards him. Then he knew it wasn't right. Each of the pilots was also wearing a parachute.

"Don't even flinch," said one of the pilots to Tank.

King woke up then, so did Blade and Salt. King turned around and looked to see the one pilot blocking the hallway on the far side of the toilet.

"Don't fucking move, not even an inch," the pilot said to King.

The second pilot was opening the door. Tank looked at his watch; the altimeter was reading just under ten thousand feet. "At this altitude, the pressure difference shouldn't be too bad," he thought.

With a whoosh, the door opened and the air in the cabin rushed out quickly. Tank watched his unread Asimov's magazine fly out as if possessed. Then the smell of Africa and the cool night air came in as the pressures equalized.

"Die bravely, American pawns," said one of the pilots in Russian. Not only did the four of them know enough Russian to understand what he was saying, the pilot's demeanor would have given it away in any event.

His English accent was perfect. His Russian took everyone by surprise. The pilot pointed his gun menacingly at King and his men before disappearing past the paneling of the toilet and out the open door.

King jumped up.

"Get the parachutes, just in case, I'm heading in to see if we can't fly this plane to our destination," he said.

"Man," said Tank, "the only American in our midst is you, and we get lumped in."

Tank grinned, Blade laughed out loud and Salt smirked. They all jumped up and made their way to the back of the plane to grab the parachutes from their gear.

King rushed into the cockpit to grab control of the plane. It was on autopilot. That was a small relief. He took a look at the controls before deciding to take over. Just as he was about to disengage autopilot a flashing red dot caught his eye.

Just under the main instrument panel on the co-pilot's side, where his feet would have been, King saw a bomb. It was probably C-4. It was encased in a plastic box, which was bolted to the floor. There was maybe a pound's worth and it had an electronic timer detonation. The timer was counting down. Fifty-three seconds, fifty-two seconds. King didn't need to watch the clock.

He leapt out of his seat and ran down the hallway to the back of the plane.

"Thirty seconds!" he yelled. "A bomb in the cockpit is going off. Grab what you can carry and jump."

The others needed no encouraging. They all grabbed their own personal rucksacks and put them on over their chests.

They already had their parachutes on. All three of them grabbed HK416 carbines and slung them over their shoulders.

They were leaving two large duffel bags behind with a lot of useful gear. But they couldn't think of that right now. What they grabbed were the essentials.

King slung his parachute over his shoulders and clipped it together around his chest. He didn't bother with the leg straps. Tank helped him into his rucksack, which he put over his chest. His HK416 was slung over his chest too.

"Let's roll," he said over the noise of the outside night air rushing past the door.

They all dove out, one after the other. Salt then Blade, then Tank and then King. King looked back as the plane flew on. He pulled his cord and the parachute opened and buffeted him vertical. Above him, but off to the south there was a big fiery explosion.

He saw the explosion in yellows and oranges before he heard it. And with the sound came the shock wave, which jostled all of them as they fell like shadows from the night sky. Then it got very quiet.

May 7, 2012 1:33 a.m.

Somewhere inside Cameroon

By the light of the moon and some flashlights, King and his team repacked their parachutes. They didn't want to leave anything out here for anyone to find. King didn't have a clue who the pilots had turned out to be and he wanted to find out. Did they know who King and TaXI worked for? Did they know about ANA? These were questions he wanted answers to.

By King's counting he figured that the pilots were probably north of his location by about fifteen to twenty kilometers. That wasn't much. Blade, Tank and Salt gathered around King.

"I want us to hike to the wreckage to see if we can find anything salvageable," said King. "I don't know where we are, but we're well inside Cameroon. Blade?"

Blade took out his tablet and connected it to a secure satellite linkup. It was slower than fiber and data, but much faster than dial up. Within several seconds he had pin pointed their exact location.

"We're just over ten kilometers north of Yaoundé. Three hours maximum if we give it a leisurely hike. Quicker if we go faster," said Blade.

"As long as we get there before daybreak, I'm happy," said King. "Blade, can you pinpoint where the G-V is?"

"Yeah, I've got it right here," said Blade, pointing to a blue dot on the map. "At least the part that held the black box is there."

Salt, Tank, Blade and King were all huddled around the seven-inch tablet Blade was holding.

"Give me terrain," said King.

Blade punched some buttons on the screen and a satellite image of the terrain came up.

"Good, I want us heading up this way," said King, pointing to an area that was full of bushes and trees. "That way we stay covered. I have a suspicion those clowns flying us earlier are probably being picked up as we speak."

The team nodded in agreement.

"I want us to stay covered and we're going in dark," said King.

"Understood," said Tank.

Salt and Blade nodded. Blade took a reading off the Southern Cross, found south and followed it to the horizon where a particular lonely tree was just about dead center for him to follow. He turned off the tablet and put it away.

Everyone turned off their flashlights and put those away, too. They pulled out their night vision goggles and put them on. They were now nothing more than inky shadows in the warm Cameroon night as they set out almost due south, zig zagging in between bushes and trees.

The going was slower than King was hoping. But they were carrying over fifty pounds of gear, each man. This included the HK416 Carbines, the Beretta M9s, lots of ammo, including JHP 9mm rounds for the Beretta as well as several magazines for the HK416s.

King thought he heard something. He brought his hand up and his team stopped behind him. He pulled his hand down and they all got into a crouch.

King listened quietly. It was the sound of a truck or car engine. He reached into his pack and brought up his night vision binoculars. He pointed them towards the truck he could see coming.

It was an older safari truck and it was barreling down on them fast. King pushed his arms backward and they all squirmed further into the brush and bushes. The truck didn't have its headlights on. That was smart. They were being stealthy.

The truck came by, about fifteen feet from the TaXI team. King noticed the driver was a black man, probably Cameroonian. He was wearing green army fatigues and a beret. In the passenger seat was the first officer who had flown them not an hour before. The back seat held the co-pilot and in the middle, standing, was another black Cameroonian manning a machine gun on a turret. The truck had no roof.

The man on the back was pointing towards the horizon and yelling to the driver in French. They didn't notice TaXI, it would have been hard. The men were well camouflaged.

King stood up and watched after them, looking through the binoculars.

On the horizon in the distance was a soft smoldering fire. He zoomed in on it and the binoculars read 1,100 meters.

King pointed at the horizon. Even without the night vision binoculars you could see the smoldering fire and the gray smoke smudging against the inky black sky.

"Eleven hundred meters," said King. "Double speed, I want to consult our friends."

Tank chuckled softly.

"Yeah, I'd like to have words with them too," he said.

They got up and started off at a strong, fast walk. The night sky was warm. They were starting to sweat when they finally made it to the debris. Most of it had landed within a hundred meter radius. The fuselage was mostly in two pieces. A smaller chunk which had been the cockpit and the larger rear section. The wings were in pieces and not attached to the plane.

The debris had landed in an open area. There were clumps of large bushes just on the perimeter of the debris field. A couple of taller trees were dotted around.

King and his team crept in quietly towards the perimeter, staying under cover of the thick bushes. They lined up, each on one knee, and watched the Cameroonians and Russians walking around the debris looking at things here and there. The TaXI team was about thirty meters from where the main fuselage and the Cameroonian's truck were.

Salt took off his carbine and steadied it with his elbow on one knee. He sighted and drew on the Cameroonian who had been manning the gun turret in the truck.

"Permission to kill, Colonel?" he asked King. King nodded.

"Make it clean. Take out both Cameroonians if you can. I want the Russians alive. Disable the truck after you've taken out the Cameroonians."

The Russian first officer was kneeling down. He was picking up what looked like the black box. He was saying something to the Cameroonian driver. The other Cameroonian was off with the co-pilot investigating the main fuselage section several meters away from where the first officer was.

Salt steadied his carbine and adjusted his scope. He would have preferred having his sniper rifle with him.

But this trip wasn't like that. It wasn't supposed to be an assassination and those sniper rifles were to heave to carry around. All things considered, on this occasion he was glad he didn't actually have his Dragunov SVD.

At thirty meters if he was worth his salt, pun intended, this should be an easy kill. He drew a breath and steadied himself. The Russian was passing the black box to the Cameroonian. Salt put his finger gently on the trigger. He had a clear shot right into the temple. Salt gently squeezed the trigger like he was pressing clay. The shot was loud. He saw the red mist on the side of the Cameroonian's head and then he dropped dead.

It was a good, clean hit. Salt allowed just a small smile. All hell broke lose. There was shouting and scurrying. The first officer leapt to his feet and ran to the truck. The co-pilot was with him. The remaining Cameroonian was looking in the TaXI team's direction.

The first officer jumped into the driver's seat. The engine on the truck was idling. The co-pilot jumped in next to him and the Cameroonian took his place in the back.

He grabbed the machine gun on the turret and swiveled it around violently. The Cameroonian started firing indiscrimanently as the truck started off.

He was firing in TaXI's general direction, but blindly; the bullets chewing into the ground several meters to the left of TaXI, spitting up clumps of dirt and vegetation. The truck hit a bump and the Cameroonian bounced in the back, snaking his machine gun up and over the TaXI team's head.

Salt steadied himself again. This time he needed to be quicker. He looked through the scope, took a breath. A chest shot would offer more room for error. He zeroed in on his target and squeezed the trigger. A puff of red erupted from the Cameroonian's chest like a blossoming flower. It wasn't dead center, it was even better. Salt's bullet had drilled slightly left into his chest, probably bursting his heart like a popped water balloon.

Salt steadied again and scoped for the back of the truck, looking for the gasoline tank.

He found it and slowly squeezed the trigger. Just as he did, a hyrax brushed past him, a large cat-like creature looking like a squirrel, and his shot went wide.

The truck was darting off, gaining speed. The two Russians were probably closing in on a hundred meters now, making it too dangerous to disable the truck without risking injury or death to either of the Russians.

King brought up his hand in front and to the right of Salt. Salt nodded.

"Too far," Salt said.

"Agreed," said King. "Good shooting otherwise."

He patted Salt on the back and the four of them stood up and made their way to the wreckage.

Their duffel bags were strewn all about and nothing worth salvaging was in any shape to be salvaged. Most of it was broken and burned beyond use. King and his team picked through what they could, but nothing they wanted or needed could be found.

There were still some small fires burning eagerly.

"Let's get rid of a few pounds," King said. "We'll leave our parachutes here. Being on the ground, I can't think we'll need them again soon. And we've got a long walk ahead of us."

Salt went over to the first man he had shot. He rifled through his pockets and found some ID. He flipped it open. It was Cameroon Army identification and the man's name was Elvis Ngwa.

Tank had caught up with the dead machine gunner. He had fallen out of the back of the truck as it sped away. Tank found his identification, the same as his fallen friend's. He was also Cameroonian Army. His name was Cheo Ndi.

Tank walked over to Salt and they checked out each other's found IDs.

"What's Cameroonian Army doing with the Russians?" Tank asked as he showed the ID to King and Blade as they all huddled together.

"That's a question I'd like to know the answer to," said King.

"I'd also like to know why the pilots wanted us dead," said Blade. "They didn't expressly say they knew we were TaXI."

King nodded.

"That's true, but they were on an ANA plane so they must have known. At least that's my belief.

But how much they know about our assignment is something I want the answer to. And if they're looking out for Bembe we might have our work cut out for us. Let's be prepared for more unfriendlies," said King. "Blade, how much further?"

King looked at his watch, it was coming up on 2 a.m. Blade took out his tablet and started it up.

"Where we headed, Colonel?" asked Blade.

"Military supply. I want to get some wheels for our trip down to Angola," answered King.

Blade zoomed into the map. Searched for any army outposts and found the closest one to them, just on the outskirts of Yaoundé. It was a smaller army base. Something they might have better luck at infiltrating.

"This one here," said Blade, showing everyone, "looks close and small enough for us to sneak in and out of."

King nodded.

"I like it," King said.

"It's just under eight clicks, King," said Blade.

"Good. Let's go team. I want us there before 4 a.m.," said King.

TA.X.I. TO ANGOLA

May 7, 2012 3:57 a.m.

Somewhere outside Yaoundé, Cameroon

King and his team crept up through the bushes. The trees and shrubs were thicker here on the outskirts of Yaoundé and he was grateful for that. They didn't have unlimited supplies of ammunition, and only a few hand grenades and flashbangs. They had kept up a good pace and he was happy to be here under thick brush.

The night sky was slowly, very slowly, starting to lighten. It was still a dark navy blue, but the black of night was starting to wake up. He halted his men and crouched down. He brought out his night vision binoculars and looked through a clearing in front of him.

Five hundred meters ahead was the outer perimeter of the Cameroonian Presidential Palace grounds.

Dotted just around the perimeter wall and closest to King and his men were half a dozen large metal buildings. They likely held army surplus. King thought about it for a moment. This was closer to them than the army base they were heading for, which was another kilometer or two from their position to the west.

King turned around and looked at his team.

"What say we try for those buildings there," said King, pointing behind him. "They might be more heavily protected, being part of the Presidential Palace, but they're much closer."

Blade nodded his head.

"I agree," said Blade, "no need to look a gift horse in the mouth."

Salt and Tank nodded in agreement.

"Good," said King, "let's go."

They all followed him, crouching and creeping behind thick brush and trees. They came up to an opening. There was about a thirty meter perimeter around the first building that was open.

King nodded to Salt. Salt nodded back. He lay down beside a bush and trained his carbine on the building. He was going to stay behind and offer cover in the event things went sideways.

It was just after four, still dark. King and Blade and Tank surveyed the area through their night vision goggles. Just behind the main door at the first building there was a man smoking a cigarette. He didn't appear to be armed. He was likely maintenance.

King looked at Blade and with hand gestures instructed him to disable the man. He adamantly ordered that he not be killed. They had no qualms with the Cameroonians other than the first two they had earlier killed.

King gestured for Tank and him to enter the building and the three of them took off towards the building. The moon was now low on the horizon, behind the building. This gave them even greater cover of night. Blade led the way, followed by King, with Tank bringing up the rear.

The Cameroonian had just flicked his cigarette to the ground and was about to step it out when Blade came up behind him, just rounding the corner of the building. King and Tank held back, watching for anyone else.

Blade, being much taller than the Cameroonian, quickly got him into a sleeper hold.

He squeezed firmly until the man slumped back in his arms. Blade dragged him into the building, following King and Tank as they entered. Tank had the syringe ready with the anesthetic. The sleeper hold only gave them several seconds.

Tank stuck the needle in the man's brachial artery just as he was starting to stir. He was knocked out right away, sleeping like a baby.

The building was even darker than outside. Only a row of glass windows about twenty feet high, covered in dust, never cleaned, let in any light. The building was mostly empty, but at the far end was a tarp covering what looked like an army truck.

King ran up to it and with the help of Tank they pulled off the tarp. To King's delight, underneath was the newest Marauder. An armored military vehicle that could carry up to ten.

"Hell, yeah!" exclaimed Tank.

King tried the passenger door, it was open. He climbed in. Blade climbed in the back and Tank climbed in the front.

Tank was looking at the steering column, trying to figure out how to start it up. How he might hotwire this big truck.

"Did you try the visor for the keys?" asked King.

Tank looked up at him and raised his eyebrows.

"Don't be stupid," Tank said.

"I'm just saying," said King and he flipped down the visor where a set of keys fell into Tank's lap.

"Who does that, really?" said Tank. It wasn't really a question.

"Well, apparently a lot of people," said King. "I've seen it plenty of times on the movies."

Suddenly, King heard shouting. There was an office up on a second level of this building, looking over the general area they were in. They had overlooked it when they saw the truck under the tarp.

"Best be going," said King.

Tank grabbed the keys and put them in the ignition and turned it over. It didn't start immediately. Blade was looking out the back door's window.

"The guy's got an AK-47," said Blade. "Anytime now would be helpful."

"Unless he's got armor piercing rounds, you should be just fine," said King.

"I'd rather not find out, thank you," said Blade.

With that, the diesel engine roared to life. Tank took a quick look at the complicated dash and pushed some buttons and flicked some levers.

"Let's get ready to rumble," said Tank.

And with that the sound of the AK-47 echoed and roared as the man landed on the main level, having climbed down the stairs from his office. The bullets pinged and ricocheted off the armor plating, sounding very much like a pinball machine or a slot machine offering winnings.

"We have a winner," said King.

The tires squealed on the slick concrete floor and then the Marauder lurched forward.

"Straight through the door and through the park, please, Jeeves," said King smirking.

"My pleasure, Colonel," said Tank as he laughed aloud.

The Marauder punched through the aluminum roll up door as if it was driving through paper.

Tank drove up beside the bush where Salt was getting up, grinning like a kid at Christmas as he saw the Marauder come lurching out of the building.

Tank slowed down to a crawl but didn't stop. Blade swung the back door open as Salt ran for it. The Cameroonian came out and pointed the rifle at the Marauder, Tank turned the Marauder ninety degrees to offer some protection to Salt as the AK-47 chewed up the dusty ground around him and bullets pinged off the open door.

Salt jumped in and Blade closed the door behind him. Tank put his foot to the floor and the Marauder's tires dug into the ground and it grunted forward, picking up speed, fast for its size. The bullets continued for a few seconds, mostly missing, some clanging like tin cups against the Marauder's tough shell. Then they stopped.

Salt looked back out the window and saw the Cameroonian on his cell phone, waving his AK-47 up and down in the air.

"I think we're gonna have company in a minute," Salt said.

Tank was going as fast as he could. The Marauder was cruising along at one hundred kilometers per hour. Tank made his way around the Presidential Palace and onto the N1. There was no sign of anyone following them just then.

He continued along the N1 until it joined up with N2. The roads were practically empty but the sky was beginning to lighten slowly. The navy blue was turning French blue.

"Get us off these main roads as soon as you can, Tank," said King. "Blade, give us a hand here."

Blade pulled out his tablet again and searched for the path less trodden.

"There's not much available, King, until we get past the airport. That's about twenty kilometers still. But after that we can cut west out into the brush and out of sight."

King nodded.

"Keep us posted, Blade. Tank, I want us off these main roads as soon as Blade gives direction."

Tank nodded. His face was calm but focused. Driving a fifteen ton vehicle at a hundred kilometers per hour took determined concentration.

"What's our fuel like?" asked King.

Tank looked at the gauge and tapped it for King to look at.

"Full tank, King," said Tank, "should get us about seven hundred clicks."

King smiled.

"The Cameroonians have been most hospitable, but it's about 1,600 clicks to Luanda isn't it, Blade?" asked King.

"Less than that as the crow flies," said Blade, "but probably around that for us. We'll need at least two more fill ups."

King nodded. The road before them was dark but the moon was still out, giving ample illumination for them to see through their night vision goggles. They had not turned on the headlights and that's exactly how they wanted it.

"We've got company," said Salt.

"Man the machine gun, if you will, Major," said King.

Salt climbed up and moved into position to access the machine gun. It was pointing forward, which is not where the Cameroonians were coming from.

Salt turned the machine gun around and focused on them. There were four small army vehicles. The same kind that the Russians had been in before. They looked like URIs.

They had a driver, a passenger, and a man standing up pointing a medium caliber machine gun at them. It was a fair fight. Salt reckoned the machines guns on their trucks were the same as his.

"We're looking to minimize casualties here, Salt," said King. "We have no argument with the Cameroonians."

"Understood, Colonel," said Salt.

The four Cameroonian vehicles were gaining on them. Their lights were bright; Salt adjusted his night vision goggles to compensate. One benefit he had over them were the night vision goggles. And of course, his renowned marksmanship abilities.

The URIs were about a hundred meters when the first of them started firing away. Tracer ammo zipped by, chewed the pavement behind the Marauder like laser pins or shooting stars. Though these weren't wishing the TaXI team well.

"No need to encourage them, Salt," said King. "Quick work if you don't mind."

"I'm a sniper, Colonel, not a butcher," said Salt.

He brought up the machine gun barrel and aimed steadily. The Marauder was bouncing around on the bad roads of Cameroon as Salt tried to aim for the tires of the front vehicle.

"A little help here," Salt said turning back to look down at Tank.

"It's not me, it's the road," replied Tank.

Salt paid no attention. He squeezed the trigger to let go a stream of silver bullets that looked like ribbons. His mark was too low, the bullets dug and spat along the road. The Cameroonians were gaining on him.

He didn't mind that. The closer they came, the better his chances of disabling them without causing many casualties. Though conversely, the better their chances of hitting him.

He ducked down behind the gun, trying to aim along the barrel as best as he could. He breathed deeply. Felt the trigger under his finger and waited for a moment.

The road was as smooth as it was going to be. Salt squeezed and let go another ribbon of bullets. He saw them spark against the radiator along the driver's side and find their mark on the driver's front wheel. The tire came completely off the rim.

The rim dug into the pavement and the URI pulled hard to the driver's left. Just as it was driving off the road one of the trucks behind it slammed on its brakes and nosed right into the side of it. The rear truck's backend lifted up and the truck flipped over the first one and landed upside down. The first truck was tossed onto its side and skidded into the dust and dirt on the side of the road. The machine gunner from the rear truck was ejected but landed safely on a soft clump of thick bushes.

The remaining two URIs careened past the upside down truck and continued their menacing approach towards the Marauder.

These two trucks were side by side, their four headlights like two monsters bearing down on Salt. The machine gunners squeezed their triggers and tracers of light zipped on by and pinged against the Marauder's shell.

Some bullets zipped too closely by Salt, one of them ricocheting off the roof inches from where he was positioned, ejecting a fragment of bullet that sliced his left cheek. It was a flesh wound, but it smarted and started to bleed.

Salt gritted his teeth. The Cameroonians were no more than thirty meters back. He had to make these next shots count or he might as well duck back into the cover of the Marauder rather than stay out here for easy pickings.

He steadied himself and looked down the barrel. He was about to pull the trigger when the Marauder bounced off a pothole. Salt lost his balance and almost slipped off the ledge that he stood on to access the machine gun.

"That's not helping!" Salt yelled.

Tank ignored him.

"Chin up, Salt," said King, "you can do it. I have all the faith in the world."

Salt eased himself back down to steady his aim. He leaned back against the hole in the roof to brace himself better. He lined up the barrel and sighted in.

The Cameroonians were unloading another volley of lead at him. He felt the bullets zinging past him and ricocheting off the roof. "This is your last chance," he thought to himself.

He lined up his approach. He was going for the truck on his left first and then he'd zip across to the right. He steadied, breathed and waited. He felt good. The Marauder was racing along steadily.

Salt squeezed the trigger and held it. The machine gun was shaking his hands vigorously, like a happy handshake to seal a deal well done. The bullets zipped past the first truck but found their mark as he gripped the gun more firmly. He pulled it slowly across his right and all four front tires of the two remaining URIs blew up and came off the rims.

He watched the trucks lose control and each veered into the ditch nearest them before slowly falling over onto their sides.

"Woohoo," said Blade, who had been watching through the back window.

Salt ducked back down into the back and took his seat.

"That's good shooting, soldier," said Blade.

Salt smiled, and wiped the blood off his cheek.

"You need something for that?" asked Blade.

Salt shook his head.

"Let me look," said Blade.

Blade looked at the flesh wound and it was indeed just that. He put some tape over it after wiping it with an antiseptic cloth.

"We're just coming past the airport," said Tank.

"Right," said Blade, grabbing his tablet. "Just a hundred meters veer off to the right at about a fifteen degree angle. You should see it. It'll be a clearing. Stay on that path for a bit."

Tank nodded and took the path less trodden as it came into view.

TA.X.I. TO ANGOLA

May 7, 2012 6:06 p.m.

President's Palace Luanda, Angola

Two white men jumped out of a truck followed by two black Angolans. The men walked briskly up to the palace gates where they were met by armed military guards. They flashed their badges and a guard opened up a small door in the gate through which the four of them passed.

The white men walked in front of the two black men. Nobody was speaking. The faces on the two white men were dour.

Things had not gone as they had planned. They walked up the steps and into the stately, colonial building. An assistant met them.

"Follow me," she said in Portuguese. "The President is expecting you."

They followed her as she rushed down the long hallway, up some stairs to the second level. Then she rushed down the hallway and halted at the end of it where two large wooden doors were closed. She knocked.

The doors were opened by a large black Angolan wearing army clothes. He smiled at her, showing a gap between his two front teeth. He moved aside and stretched out his right arm, inviting them in.

The five of them walked in. The two Angolans behind the two white men carried pistols in side holsters. The large Angolan who had opened the door was unarmed. But, on either side of the door facing a large wooden desk behind which sat the President, were two Angolans armed with AK-47s and pistols.

The two white men looked around nervously. Sweat stained their underarms.

"Welcome, gentleman," said President Serge Vincente with outstretched hands. "Please sit down."

The two men sat down and tried their best to offer a smile.

"Thank you for seeing us on such short notice," said the one man in Portuguese with a Russian accent.

"Not at all. Not at all," said the President.

He was still smiling at them, but his eyes were hard, like crushed coal.

The second seated man looked at the first one and swallowed hard.

"We… we have some bad news, President," he said in Portuguese, through a Russian accent.

"Tell me, Mr. Tomas Balabanov," said the President.

"Well… um, the Americans did not die in the plane crash," the co-pilot of the ANA G-V said.

The President gritted his teeth and clenched his jaw. It was hot in the Presidential Palace, the air conditioning wasn't working, and yet a chill ran up Balabanov's spine.

"I'm afraid they fired on us when we went to look over the wreckage. I am sure that they'll be heading this way, still. They killed two of our men," said the first officer.

"Mr. Alex Isayev," said the President, addressing the first officer. "I paid you ten million dollars with clear instructions that TaXI was to be destroyed, and you bring me bad news."

The President stood up.

"Tell me why I should let you live when you have failed your mission," the President said slamming his fist against the table.

"Bembe cannot be taken hostage and tried for war crimes. The stability of the Angolan government requires his expertise. And we can only count on his expertise if he is around," said the President staring at the Russians.

The expertise that the President was talking about was his methods of torture and keeping the democratic uprising in check.

The two armed guards at the back of the room came forward, one beside each of the Russians. They pulled out their pistols, and pointed them at the Russians' temples.

"Let's not be unreasonable," said Isayev. "We said we'd kill them and we will. We just came to let you know. We will finish what we started."

"Yes, you will," said the President, waving away the two armed guards. "And you will take two of my best guards with you to ensure you finish the job."

"Thank you, President," said Balabanov. "You won't be disappointed."

The Russians got up to leave.

"There is one more thing," said the President, looking at them.

"Anything," said Isayev.

"You have twenty four hours, at which time I want TaXI dead and nine million of my ten million dollars returned for underperformance of your duties," said the President.

President Vincente looked at them with hard, cruel eyes.

"But, President..." protested Balabanov.

The President waived him to silence.

"I will have my money back. You can keep one million dollars as a good faith gesture from me that you will now succeed," said the President.

"And if we don't bring the money back?" asked Isayev, afraid of the answer.

"If you don't," said the President smiling at him, "then your widows will enjoy the money."

The Russians nodded and the President waved them out.

TA.X.I. TO ANGOLA

May 7, 2012 12:12 p.m.

Inside Gabon not far from the border with Congo

King was pleased with how well his men had been doing on this African safari, so far. They had crossed the border between Cameroon and Gabon without incident. It had taken a bit of time to determine a suitable entry, but unlike the American border with Mexico, most African borders were non-descript and border patrol all but non-existent. Still, you had to be careful, as patrols would appear every couple of hours or so.

Just inside Gabon, they had to jump back on the N2 briefly in order to cross the Ntem River. But the river crossing guards were quite happy with a two hundred dollar toll offered by Tank to allow for crossing.

They had managed to siphon off some diesel from an idling truck parked just behind a beaten down building in one of the smaller towns in Gabon. The brick, whitewashed building was flaking paint like dandruff onto the ground around its perimeter. And the once smart, shiny, metal roof was rusting and corroding in parts.

Blade was pumping out the diesel when the driver came back out, yelling and screaming. TaXI didn't need to draw any negative attention to them, so they took off having only taken a few gallons.

Tank kept looking at the fuel gauge nervously. It was leaning precariously just above the empty line. The Cameroonians had been extremely helpful. Not only with the full tank of diesel that the Marauder had started off with, but with the addition of the two plastic gas cans attached, one on each side of the back. The petroleum gods had smiled on them, from all the fire they had taken, the gas cans had not been hit except for a bullet hole on the upper quarter which hardly leaked any fuel. They had been full when the Marauder left Cameroon, but they were now empty. Their five-gallon insides containing nothing more than the aroma of their former contents.

The Congo is a thickly forested area and the driving was difficult. Tank was on his second driving duty. They were driving in one to two hour shifts. The day had bloomed hot and humid like the inside of a wet blanket warmed in the oven. King, Blade, Salt and Tank were blistered with sweat.

Tank liked it, though. The hot weather was much better than the cold he'd experienced in Maryland. He was grateful for that.

The Marauder had no air conditioning and they wouldn't have been using it either. They needed every drop of fuel to get them as far as possible. Stopping and refueling unnecessarily was just inviting trouble.

"Give me an ETA to the border, Blade," said King, still sitting in the passenger seat.

Blade looked at his tablet.

"We're about 63 kilometers from the Congo border, Colonel," said Blade.

King nodded and wiped the sweat from his brow.

"Anybody got any water left?" he asked.

He was met with negative murmurs.

"As soon as we've crossed over," said King, "we need to find two things. Diesel and water."

King looked over at Tank. His jaw was clenched; he was driving through the forest staying parallel to the P7 road that would take them into Congo. Sometimes they had to veer onto it in order to make up time. Sometimes, the thicket of forest was too much and too slow going. They had made great time considering, but they needed to keep their speed up.

"How far do you think we have with the fuel left, Tank?" asked King.

Tank glanced down at the fuel gauge. It was a few millimeters above the empty line. But he reckoned empty only happened a few millimeters below the empty line. At least that had been his experience with military vehicles.

He glanced over at King for just a moment before looking back out the front windshield. Off to King's right you could see the P7 road. It wasn't paved, but it was graded reasonably well. There weren't many vehicles on it, and that's one of the reasons they'd chosen this route. In the last hour they'd counted maybe three vehicles. Two small trucks and one car.

"I figure maybe we've got two hundred clicks left. And that's including fumes, if we're lucky," said Tank.

Tank rubbed his lower right cheek and jaw against his shoulder as a wet snake of sweat rolled down his temple, causing an itch.

"We might be walking the rest of the way to Luanda, gentlemen," said King smirking.

"Unless we cut west onto the N3 which will expose us, but give us a better shot at finding diesel," said Blade.

King nodded, so did Tank.

"We have no choice, King," said Salt. "I didn't come out here to do a walking safari, either."

Tank chuckled.

"Ain't that the truth," he said.

"Then that's what we'll do," said King.

TA.X.I. TO ANGOLA

May 7, 2012 4:54 p.m.

Inside the Congo 10 kilometers from Dolisie

Thank God for the N3, a paved road that had taken them through some very nice nature reserves and had delivered TaXI to a gas station where they had been able to fill up the tank with diesel.

Against his better judgment, King had agreed with the rest of his team to stay on the paved road at least through to Dolisie, the third largest city in Congo.

Congo had been relatively democratic for an African nation since 1992. The thing that concerned King was Congo's general ambivalence to foreigners of both European and American descent.

Ambivalence was difficult to deal with. He much preferred knowing where he stood, whether hated or loved, rather than trying to figure it out as he went. An additional concern was bribery. Having not planned on being derailed, TaXI had not brought along much money for bribery. They had roughly five hundred dollars left amongst the four of them, which was not going to stretch very far. They had to get through Congo as well as the Democratic Republic of the Congo before they were home free, to a degree, in Angola.

Salt was seated to King's left now. He was up driving. Something he hated. Not that he was a bad driver, he just didn't like the concentration and the focus required. He much preferred working with smaller items. Like guns and knives and other assorted tools of his trade.

It was hotter in the Marauder than it was outside. Even with all the vents open and the gun turret opened wide, the air was barely moving inside the Marauder. Blade's thermometer was reading just over 35 Celsius inside the truck. Back at the gas station it had been 32 in the shade.

Blade and Tank, in the back of the Marauder were in their vests, still mostly damp with sweat. Salt, up front, had his shirt unbuttoned over a vest, the same as King. The sky was blue, dotted with puffy balls of white clouds. The N3 was a busier road and steady traffic was keeping them company. The Marauder was hogging most of its lane, but this highway was more than wide enough for it.

Salt took his hand off the steering wheel and pointed forward. King nodded his head.

"I see it," said King.

"Looks like we've got company," said Salt.

Up ahead about half a kilometer was an army checkpoint. There were more than a dozen Congolese army men in their finest army green. There were half a dozen army trucks dotted on either side of the road and large cement Jersey barriers were placed in a line pointing upwards towards the oncoming traffic.

These traffic barriers created an inverted funnel through which only one vehicle could pass at a time.

There were only half a dozen vehicles up ahead which had slowed to a crawl as a Congolese army man was frantically trying to wave them past as he clutched his machine gun with this left hand.

"I reckon we could bust through those Jersey barriers pretty easily, Colonel," said Salt. "Are you game?"

King shook his head.

"No, we've got no beef with the Congolese. I'm expecting a bit of chit chat and then we'll be well on our way again."

As the last of the cars slipped through the narrow opening of the barricade, the Congolese army soldier stood in the middle of the opening with his right hand up in the universal sign for "stop".

Off to the side, another soldier hoisted to his shoulder an RPG with grenade already attached. King didn't like the look of that.

"Do you want me on the turret?" asked Tank.

King again shook his head.

"I don't think he's going to use it. He looks too relaxed. It's meant to be threatening and nothing more."

"If you say so," said Blade.

Blade and Tank were leaning in from their seats in the back, attached to each side. More of the soldiers were getting into position. Several had knelt down behind the Jersey barriers with their weapons aimed and ready at the encroaching Marauder.

"Fuck," spat Salt, "this is the last thing we need."

"Easy," said King. "Let's not get our knickers in a knot before we know what's really going on here."

Salt pulled the Marauder to a stop about twenty feet in front of the soldier who still had his hand up.

"Do you think this was created just for us?" asked Blade in the back.

"Yeah, I'm afraid it's looking quite likely," said King.

"Someone probably called it in," said Tank. "I mean who drives a Marauder down the main highway without bringing attention to themselves."

From behind the soldier, who was just now bringing his hand down, stepped forward a fat Congolese man with nothing more than a pistol on his belt. He walked up to the driver's side of the vehicle, keeping a distance of about ten feet from Salt's door. He was smiling genially but his left hand was on his pistol.

"Get out of the vehicle," he bellowed in French.

Salt looked at King and then at Blade and Tank.

"My French is rusty," said Salt. "A little help.

"He wants us to exit the vehicle," said Blade.

"Well, what do you say, Colonel?" asked Salt.

"Let's stretch our legs," said King. "I could use a little walkabout. Remember, let's be congenial and easy going unless provoked otherwise. I don't like the numbers here. Let's be smart."

King lingered a look at Salt. Salt looked back at him.

"What?" said Salt.

"You know what," said King. "Keep an easy, peaceful feeling."

He smiled at Salt and Salt grinned back.

"Scout's honor," he said, holding up the three finger salute.

They all got out of the vehicle slowly. King first, then Salt exited from the driver's side. Blade and Tank exited the back where they were welcomed by three Congolese soldiers pointing AK-47s at their chests. The TaXI team kept their arms up around shoulder height as they were all disarmed of their Berettas.

"Where are you from, and what are you doing here?" asked the fat soldier in French, when they were all huddled around him by the front of the Marauder.

"We don't speak French," said King smiling softly.

Already, there was a line of traffic gathering behind the Marauder, in front of a Congolese soldier with his arm out stopping the traffic.

"Ah, Americans," said the fat soldier in English this time. "I am General Armand Kihoussa of the Congolese Army."

The General was still smiling warmly, but there was something about this tone that wasn't making King feel warm and tingly inside.

"Who are you and what are you doing here?" the General asked again. His English was perfect with a slight British accent to it.

"I am Kade King, this is Bain Blade," said King pointing to his left, and then to his right. "And that is Sun Salt and next to him is Taye Tank."

"And why are you here?" asked the General.

"Well, we're actually trying to get to Luanda. We are supposed to be conducting a training exercise with the Angolan military, but our plane had problems and we had to land rather abruptly in Cameroon."

The General nodded.

"The Cameroonians alerted us to their missing truck," said the General, looking past King at the Marauder sitting squat and contentedly, like a large well fed rhino. The General's eyes drifted back to King.

"Do you have identification?" he asked.

King nodded.

"In our right cargo pockets you'll find our passports."

The General nodded at one of his men who came up to King and took out his passport.

He did the same with the other three's passports too. The soldier didn't open them, but rather he demurely gave them to the General.

The General opened up the top one, which was, King's. He looked at the picture and then he looked back at King.

"Yes," said the General, "this is you."

Then he opened up the other passports each in turn. When he was satisfied, he gave them back to the soldier who had taken them from the TaXI team.

"So," said the General, "you are all Americans, then."

King wasn't sure if that was a question or a statement. And if it was a statement, he didn't know how to take it. There was some undercurrent in the General's voice that seemed malicious. Like a coiled cobra, looking peaceful but ready to strike.

King nodded his head. The smile on his face was hurting and starting to crack.

"Yes, General, we are Americans on our way to Angola to help the Angolan army with a training exercise."

The General held King's gaze for a while. Neither man offering any quarter to the other. Like two Chess Kings left alone on the board.

The stalemate lasted several seconds. Salt shifted on his feet and that drew the General's attention away from King.

"Yes, we will see about that," said the General.

Then he looked at one of his soldiers.

"Tie them up and take them down to the barracks and put them in cells."

He had reverted back to French. King looked at Salt and nodded. This was not the place to come undone. Their chances of survival were slim.

"I hope you understand," said the General to King while a soldier was tying King's hands together, "but I need to speak with your embassy and the Cameroonian army to determine the penalty and payment they will require for your theft of their Marauder."

King didn't say anything. He would give the Congolese people 24 hours to sort this out and allow TaXI to get back on their way. Failing that, they would free themselves if he could figure out a way.

May 8, 2012 12:12 a.m.
Dolisie, Congo

The cells weren't the worst that Blade had been in, and for Salt, who had spent some time visiting Russian Gulags, these were downright comfy. Still, King wasn't overjoyed by the fact that they were each in their own cell. Despite the fact that they had been treated reasonably well for the last seven hours in Congolese captivity, he hadn't heard from the General, and he wanted to hear from the General.

The meal they had been given around 8 p.m. wasn't bad. Mostly a plate of mashed cassava with a gravy dotted with bits of what might have been meat. It was also hot, spicy hot, but King didn't mind it. In fact, both Blade and Salt found it rather mild considering.

King was pacing up and down his cell. He did that when thinking. He was wondering why he hadn't heard from the General. He was also looking at ways to escape. He heard some clanging down the corridor, off in the distance. He went and sat back down on what was supposed to be a bed. It was a wooden board braced against the far wall on two L brackets. On top was a cheap and thin gray woolen blanket. No pillow.

King heard two sets of shoes hammering against the floor, growing slowly louder and louder. There was another clanging of opening metal doors and more footsteps hammering against the floor. Into his view came the General and an underling.

"Chair," said the General in French to the underling.

The younger man trotted off and was back in under a minute with a metal fold-out chair for the General. The General sat down and summarily dismissed the soldier with a wave of his hand, as if he was swatting away gnats.

King leaned back against the wall and watched the General.

The General reached into his shirt pocket and pulled out a packet of Gauloises cigarettes. He flipped open the lid on the blue packet and offered the filtered ends towards King.

King shook his head.

"I don't smoke," he said.

"I know," said the General in English, "it is a nasty habit. But, any man who doesn't have a vice, worries me... Colonel."

"Women and wine," said King facetiously.

The General leaned back and had a good laugh. He pulled out a cigarette and held it in his one hand while he put the packet back in his pocket. With his free hand, he reached into his pocket, stretching out his leg towards King. It looked like a huge fat sausage, tight against the General's pants.

King wondered how he knew of his rank. He had not shared that with anyone since being picked up by the Congolese. He looked steadily at the General as he flicked open his Zippo and lit his cigarette. He inhaled deeply and then blew the cigarette smoke in a careful stream towards King.

The General's pallor was not warm and healthy. Instead of the vigorous warmth of dark chestnut, the General's skin was ashen like burnt coal. Likely due to the lack of sufficient oxygen from years of smoking.

The General wheezed and coughed quickly. He talked while waving the hand holding the cigarette around, as if it were a magic wand and he the magician.

"I have spoken with the US Embassy in Brazzaville," said the General.

King didn't say anything. He watched the General steadily, as the smoke wafted into his cell. The smell was not unpleasant at its current diluted level. The General continued.

"They have no idea of who you are and why you might be here."

King still sat silently, his arms folded over his chest. The window above him was barred, but open, allowing the warm scented night air to sneak in. It smelled of fried chicken and cassava. King was pretty certain it wasn't little bits of gristled chicken that was on his dinner plate earlier.

"You do not find that surprising?" asked the General.

King shrugged.

"Bureaucrats don't know everything," he said.

The General let himself have another good chuckle before inhaling on his cigarette.

"Tell me Colonel, are you really US Army, or something else?"

"Yep, I'm really US Army," said King.

The General leaned forward and looked at King. His eyes sparked and he drew the corners of his mouth downwards in anger. But he collected himself before he spoke.

"You and I know that is not true. But it doesn't matter," said the General. "Before sunup, we will know everything we want about ANA."

"Fuck," thought King to himself. Things had just gotten more complicated than he had hoped for. That was the last thing they needed to worry about.

The General stood up. His cigarette was almost finished. He tossed it casually to the floor where he purposefully squashed it out with his foot. He did so with more deliberation and emphasis than was necessary.

"Don't get too comfortable, Colonel," said the General. "You can expect some guests within the hour, who are very eager to make your acquaintance."

TA.X.I. TO ANGOLA

May 8, 2012 12:59 a.m.

Dolisie, Congo

The two Russians were just debarking from the plane they had used to get into Congo. It hadn't been a long trip. Not by time at least, but they were eager to get everything finished. Isayev and Balabanov hadn't slept for a long time. They were tired and cranky. And they were aiming to get answers from King and his men.

"At least we still get to keep one million," said Balabanov, as the two of them stepped off the plane.

Isayev looked at him with a mixture of impatience watered down by tiredness.

"Listen," said Isayev, "we only get to keep one million if we get the job done right this time. We're going to kill them. All of them, but not before we've got some answers."

TA.X.I. TO ANGOLA

Isayev and Balabanov didn't have the highest security clearance in Moscow for this type of work. They were pawns in the greater chess being played by factions of Moscow's old Soviet guard. There were powerful people in the upper ranks of both Russia's military and government who wanted more than anything to destabilize the fragile fingers of democracy that were now already clutching the hems of Russian government and popular movements.

Angola had once been an ally, and with Bembe in place, Angola was once again going to become a crucial player in the African arena where once more the destabilization of democracy could take place.

"What kinds of questions do we want answers to?" asked Balabanov.

Balabanov was both naïve and daft when it came to political maneuverings. But he was loyal, which was the one thing that he had going for him. Isayev stopped in the middle of the tarmac and turned to his friend and comrade, putting his hands on his shoulders. He looked at him kindly, like an older brother.

"I want to find out more about these TaXI teams and about ANA," Isayev said in Russian. "If we are going to move up in the ranks of the politburo we need to have knowledge. Knowledge, comrade, is power. I will make King and his men beg to tell me everything that they know. And with this knowledge of ANA and how it is set up and funded, we will have an easier opportunity to bring it down."

Isayev turned away from Balabanov and continued to walk down the tarmac. At the far end was the General, smoking another of his Gauloises. The General waved his hand at the two Russians and Isayev returned the gesture.

"Do not trust these Russians," said the General in French, to his right hand man standing next to him.

The Congolese soldier grunted and nodded.

"We can allow them to extract information from our American guests," continued the General, "but we cannot allow them to be killed. The Americans are worth more to us alive than dead."

"Understood," said the Congolese Major.

"You are a loyal soldier, Major Lucien Kidinda," said the General as he ground out his cigarette with his shoe.

And with that, General Kihoussa walked off towards the two Russians. He reached out his right hand eagerly and both Isayev and Balabanov shook it.

"I am very glad to meet you," said the General in English. "I am looking forward to helping you debrief our American guests."

"That won't be necessary, thank you, General," said Isayev.

"But I insist," said the General, offering his toothy Cheshire grin that belied his malevolence.

"Very well," said Isayev, realizing that an argument was futile and in any event he'd deal with the meddling of these Africans later.

"Do you have any bags?" asked the General.

"No," said Isayev, "none other than this small one that my comrade Balabanov is carrying. It has our tools of the trade, you understand."

The General nodded and looked down at the small leather case that Tomas Balabanov was carrying. It was the size and color of a doctor's bag. Well worn, the leather was faded in areas and what looked like smudges of dried blood dotted the top of the enclosure.

"I look forward to learning your techniques," said the General. "Please, this way."

The General extended his arm and led the men to an older model Mercedes sedan, black in color. Major Kidinda climbed into the driver's seat and the General took the front passenger seat. Isayev and Balabanov sat in the back with the bag between them. Isayev had his arm over it as you might drape your arm over your lover's shoulder.

The Major started the car and drove away from the plane.

"Would you like to get started right away?" asked the General.

Isayev was looking out the window and thinking how much he hated Africa. A land of heat and sweat, brutality without finesse. It would be the perfect stage to destabilize democracy in the west and let the Africans pay for it. He longed for his mother Russia, the Russia of old, the Russia that the great men of Lenin and Stalin had tried so bravely to create. He turned to look at the General and he shook his head.

"No need to rush General. We will wait and bide our time. The Americans are most likely tired. I have it on good authority that they have not slept for the better part of twenty-four hours."

The General nodded.

"Tell me about this organization ANA?" asked the General.

"There is not much to tell," said Isayev, "because I do not know much, but ANA is an acronym for All Nations Alliance. Though that is capitalist propaganda. It is well known that ANA is nothing but a front for the American regime. In fact, I have seen a secret dossier issued by the American government that proves that the acronym actually means America's Nuclear Annihilation. It is a secret program to infiltrate and deposit nuclear weapons into all nations not friendly to American interests so that America might detonate and destroy these nations at will, if they deem it necessary."

Isayev looked out the window. He was a good agent he thought, smiling to himself. He had just made up that little rant on the spot. He looked back at the General who was chewing over the information in his mind. Isayev didn't care what ANA stood for or not. He wanted to know how to infiltrate it more successfully so that he and his comrades could bring it down.

"Then, it is important we get all the information from these Americans that we can.

The Congolese people will not stand for American interference on our own soil," said the General.

"We will, General, we will get everything we want out of them," said Isayev.

He stared out the window. The General was more sympathetic than he had hoped. By the time the cock crows at sunup, thought Isayev, not only will the Americans be dead, but he will have all the information he needs about ANA to make him a hero to the old guard politburo.

TA.X.I. TO ANGOLA

May 8, 2012 3:33 a.m.
Dolisie, Congo

King stirred in his sleep before he woke up. He thought he had heard Russian voices in his dream, but that seemed strange. He didn't remember dreaming, but something had woken him up.

He stood up and listened quietly for any noises. He thought he heard someone snoring. It might have been Blade or Tank. Or maybe it was one of the other prisoners in here unrelated to him. He wasn't certain where his teammates were. They had all been brought in here, but he had been placed first in one of the first cells along this long corridor.

King walked to the cell window. It was no bigger than the size of a laptop with three metal black bars thicker than a candle.

The window was about seven feet off the ground and he could see that the tops, and he imagined the bottoms, were rusting from the rain during the rainy season, which was ending this month.

King reached up and wrapped his hands around each bar on either end of the window. Then he pulled himself up and looked out. Across from him was a separate building. There was a light on, shining through the window, and he could count three heads. It was too far away to make them out clearly. Parked out front of this administration building was an older model black Mercedes. The car was not running.

King lowered himself to the floor. In the shaft of moonlight that spilled into the cell like spoiled milk he noticed flakes of black paint on his hands. He rubbed them off. He pulled himself back up, strangling the bars tightly. He shook them, but despite the rust he saw at the top where they entered the concrete, the bars were solid and immovable.

The door in the administration building opened and four men walked out. The first two were the pilot and the General.

The second pair was the co-pilot and a dark skinned Congolese soldier King had not seen before. They were walking towards the far side of the cellblock King was in. King lowered himself and reached behind him and felt the back of his belt loops.

The one thing he had appreciated about his Congolese captors was the less than stellar pat down they had given him.

They had taken his belt away, but tucked into two of the thick belt loops in the back was a handcuff key and a small knife with an extremely sharp blade. The Russians were back, and King knew that meant only one thing. They wanted him dead, but they probably wanted information first. This was going to be his only opportunity for escape. He would have to use it well.

He heard the knocking of footfalls as the four men came down the corridor. Then the clanging of the last metal door before more footfalls would bring the four of them to King's cell.

King waited and listened. He heard the clanging of the door and he figured that the Russians would want to have words with him first. He was not wrong.

The lights along the corridor and in his cell came on brightly. As bright as interrogation lights. Then the footfalls started again before ending just in front of him.

King looked up, squinting to adjust for the brightness around him. He saw the two Russians, side by side like Tweedledee and Tweedledum.

"I was wondering when you were coming back to fly me to Angola," said King smiling at the Russians.

"Arrogant American pig," spat Isayev. "I have come for you, but I am not taking you to Angola."

"Probably because they've taken your pilot's license away," said King.

Isayev's stare was hard and unflinching. Balabanov allowed himself a small smile. He liked the humor.

"Gentleman, please," said the General. "Colonel, if you'd be so kind as to put your hands through the cell so that I might cuff them. We want to have a talk with you."

King didn't move. He stood motionless at the far wall. His eyes slowly adjusting to the light. Isayev unholstered his pistol and pointed it towards King.

"It would be my pleasure to end this right now," he said.

King didn't quite believe him, but he decided not to take his chances. He walked towards the front of the cell and put his hands out between the bars in his cell door. Balabanev shook his head.

"This American pig is playing with us," he said to Isayev in Russian.

Isayev nodded.

"Colonel, please," said General, "for your own safety, do not anger these men. Put your hands through one gap so I can cuff them."

King obliged, staring at Isayev all the while. Isayev held his stare as the General handcuffed King.

"Step back, Colonel," said the General and King stepped back two paces.

The General nodded and Major Kidinda unlocked the cell's gate with one of his many keys.

"Come with us, King," said the General.

King stepped out behind the General. Behind him were the Major and the two Russians. They started walking back from where the Russian's had just come.

"When do I get to see my men?" asked King.

"Soon," said the General, not looking back.

"When do I get my phone call?" he asked smiling.

"You ask too many questions, Colonel," said the General.

They walked down another long corridor, but they did not exit the cellblock, as they might have to get to the administration building. Instead, they entered a dark, damp, and smelly building at the end. The General flicked on a light. The room had whitewashed walls that had grayed with age and misuse. It was an empty concrete block. In the middle was a wooden chair. At the back was a wash basin and table.

"Sit," ordered the General.

The Major came up behind King and pushed him towards the chair violently and sat him down on it. The Major also took some twine that Balabanov handed to him and tied King's ankles together. The General took his pistol from its holster and pointed it at King's head.

"Don't be stupid, Colonel," he said.

The Major released the handcuffs and took each of King's hands and wrapped them around the back of the chair where he cuffed them again.

"Good," said Isayev. "Now we talk."

"Tell me about your relationship with your father," said King doing his best Freudian impersonation.

TA.X.I. TO ANGOLA

May 8, 2012 3:57 a.m.

Dolisie, Congo

King couldn't breathe. It felt like the rain kept pouring down in torrents. This was supposed to be the end of the rainy season not the beginning of it. And then just as suddenly as it started, the rains stopped. The darkness lifted and King gasped for air.

"You Americans," said Isayev, holding the sopping wet cloth in front of King as it dripped onto his lap, "are ingenious at devising torture."

King breathed heavily. This was their third attempt at water boarding and he wasn't liking it.

"What do you call this technique?" asked Isayev, smiling and liking his lips.

King looked up at him and smiled back.

"We call it commie slobber," he said.

Isayev's smile dropped off his face like a porcelain plate that had just cracked. He swung the damp cloth at King's face, catching him across the left side.

"We'll do it again," said Isayev.

Balabanev grabbed King's forehead and pulled his head downwards so that his face was looking at the ceiling. Isayev placed the cloth over King's face and it stuck like cellophane. Already King was having difficulty breathing. Isayev grabbed a large jug of water and started pouring it over King's nose and mouth.

King gagged and choked and coughed. It seemed to go on for hours. And just when he couldn't take anymore and felt himself slipping into unconsciousness, it stopped.

"You are a stubborn American pig," said Isayev, as King gasped for air. "Most men give in after three waterboarding sessions. Just answer my question and this will all be over right now."

"You haven't asked me any questions," said King between breaths.

Isayev dropped the wet cloth in King's lap and shook his head.

"I have asked you to tell me who the head of ANA is," said Isayev.

"Ask nicely," said King.

Isayev punched King across the cheek, slicing him open with the ring on his right middle finger. A watery trickle of blood dripped down.

"That's better," said King.

Isayev wound up to punch King again. King grimaced in anticipation.

"Okay, wait. Wait," said King.

Isayev held his hand up in the ready.

"I'm waiting," he said.

"The head of ANA is... is Mr. Rogers," said King sincerely.

Isayev relaxed his fist and brought his hand back down to the side of his body.

"What is this Mr. Rogers first name and where is he from?" asked Isayev.

Beside him Balabanov chuckled. Isayev looked at his comrade with fiery, angry eyes. His mouth hardened to granite. Balabanov whispered something in Isayev's ear in Russian.

He turned back to King and pulled out his pistol. He pointed at his head and pulled the trigger. The noise nearly burst King's eardrum and the bullet narrowly missed his temple, hitting the far wall.

King figured it was time to start extracting himself from this situation. He began slowly, carefully, with little movement to reach for his handcuff key tucked into his back belt loop.

Isayev struck King across the temple with his pistol. Another bullet went off, narrowly missing the General before hitting the side wall.

"You make jokes when I could kill you," spat Isayev.

The blow dazed King. It cut his scalp open and watery blood began to weep from it. King focused back on his task at hand. Things were getting out of control.

"Careful," said the General to Isayev.

Isayev turned around and paced to the front of the room. He took a deep breath before turning around and coming back towards King.

"It does not matter," he said. "We have ways of making you tell the truth that do not require violence. We call it SP-118, it is far more accurate and reliable at extracting the truth than its already powerful predecessor SP-117. Furthermore, you will have no recollection of ever having spoken with me about it."

King had heard of these Russian truth serums. They were the most reliable available. In fact, when he was in Special Forces, one of the missions the Green Berets had failed at was accessing the formula for SP-117. The time for playing games was over.

King accessed the key and slowly and quietly released the handcuffs. King looked around to assess the scene. Isayev was right in front of him. To his right and a bit behind was Balabanov with arms folded. On Isayev's far left was the General, smoking a cigarette. To the General's right was the Major. The Major was menacing, he was watching King and had his right hand on the butt of his gun, which was in its holster.

Isayev reached into his bag and pulled out a syringe and a small opaque bottle with a rubber top. He plunged the needle into the bottle and turned it upside down as he siphoned the liquid into the syringe. King reached into his belt loop and pulled out the small folded knife. He slowly and carefully unfolded it.

"Now you will tell me everything that I want to know," said Isayev as he came towards King and started to lean in to give him the injection.

"You first," said King.

King swung his right arm around, sticking the end of the knife into his carotid. He pulled it out and, as Isayev staggered forward, King leapt up and circled around him. It was hard balancing with this ankles tied together, but holding onto Isayev helped. King brought his left arm under Isayev's left armpit and around his neck to help hold him up from behind. King dropped the knife and reached for Isayev's pistol, which he slipped out of its holster.

King swung his arm up as the Major was withdrawing his pistol. Two shots went off.

One from the Major's pistol and one from Isayev's pistol in King's hand. The Major's bullet hit Isayev in the stomach. King's first shot missed, ricocheting off the wall just by the Major's left ear. King fired two more shots in quick succession, realigning his aim, and both found their mark on the Major's chest like two red buttons.

The Major slumped down towards the floor, painting two red streaks of blood on the wall as he went. King released his grip on Isayev, who was losing the battle trying to plug his gushing carotid with his now slippery blood drenched hands. King fired off two more shots at the General as he desperately tried to un-holster his gun. Both made their mark with the General painting his blood against the back wall just like the Major had done before him.

King spun around to find Balabanov with his mouth wide open and his hands up in defeat. King fired off two more shots in close range, both hitting close together. Balabanov dropped to the floor with both hands still up before slumping down face first.

King hopped a pace to his left and back. He leaned down and picked up his knife and cut off the twine from his ankles. He grabbed Balabanov's gun and the Generals before grabbing the Major's set of keys and heading out to find his team.

May 8, 2012 4:14 a.m.
Dolisie, Congo

The keys clinked against the metal on the cell gate. In front of King was Blade, locked in the cell King was trying to get him out of. The first key wasn't working. The second key also wouldn't fit in the damn lock.

"Good to see you, Colonel," said Blade.

King looked up at him briefly, still fumbling with the keys.

"Not if I can't get you out of here," said King.

Down the hall could be heard several footsteps and voices shouting in French. The other guards and soldiers had been alerted and mobilized into action thanks to the bangs of the gunshots.

"Here take this just in case," said King, feeding a pistol to Blade through the cell door.

King looked to his right, from where the noise was coming from. Two Congolese soldiers were opening the far metal door. It was solid. Thankfully they couldn't shoot King through it, though he was exposed standing in the brightly lit hallway.

The third key fit into the lock and with a little jiggling it turned. King glanced down the hallway to his right. The soldiers were just opening the door. King steadied the pistol. He saw the first man come through the doorway and King fired a single shot as the soldier's rifle was being brought up to point at him. King hit him square in the heart.

The second soldier was coming in behind him, but stumbled over his fallen colleague. King fired again, but the stumbling helped the soldier narrowly avoid King's bullet. King cursed under his breath. He aimed again, quickly, as the soldier's rifle was swinging like a pendulum towards him, firing a steady stream of bullets. The second shot chewed into the soldier's shoulder and his rifle dropped flaccidly. King fired again, this time hitting him squarely in the chest.

King waited for a moment to see if there was a third soldier behind the second. There wasn't. Though he could hear many more coming from some distance.

King spun and turned the key in the lock all the way. He slid open the cell door and Blade leapt out, training his pistol down the hallway towards the dead soldiers.

"Keep lookout," said King, "while I go and release Salt and Tank."

Blade grunted his confirmation.

Down the hallway two cells down from Blade's on the opposite side was Salt.

"I have a present for you," King said as he handed Salt the third pistol he had taken.

"Thanks, Santa," said Salt, grinning at King.

King tried the first key again as he had when trying to release Blade. There were a dozen or so keys, representing, by King's estimates, the dozen or so cells down this corridor. The first didn't work. The second didn't. King didn't think the third would work having been used already to release Blade.

The fourth and then the fifth didn't work either.

"At your leisure," said Salt.

"Or I can just leave you behind," said King grinning.

Off to King's left he heard to gunshots in quick succession. He glanced up, to see a third soldier falling down on top of his comrades. Salt was squeezing his head at an angle, pressed against the bars of his cell to see what the commotion was all about.

"Good shooting," said Salt to Blade.

Blade didn't say anything. He was focused on the next soldier trying to get through the door. The pile of bodies was making it more difficult. Instead, the soldier poked his machine gun around the door and let go a stream of bullets. King dropped to the floor. Blade was too slow, and a bullet bit him as it grazed past his right shoulder. Blade cursed and dropped to one knee.

The noise was like a kitchen with cascading pots and pans falling all over the place. The bullets, clanging and banging against metal cell bars and doors. Then it stopped. The magazine was empty. The soldier withdrew his machine gun behind the door to change magazines.

King leapt to his feet and tried the sixth key, which worked. Blade ran up to the door, and straddling the dead soldiers on the floor, he put a bullet in the fourth soldier's head as he was trying to change the magazine. He dropped like a heavy sack of potatoes at Blade's feet. Blade stepped over him and looked right down the hallway. Another soldier was running towards him, trying to release the safety on his rifle. Blade steadied his pistol and fired two rounds, both erupting in small puffs of red mist on the man's shirt. He completed two more steps before tripping and falling down on his face, just feet away from Blade.

Salt was free and he came up to join Blade but not before picking up one of the AK-47s from the dead soldiers. Blade did the same with the soldier who had fallen just before him.

King started with the seventh key on Tank's cell door, which worked. He opened it up but had no presents to offer him.

"Grab a gun and let's get the hell out of here," said King.

He and Tank ran up to the far end of the hallway where Salt and Blade were crouched down watching for more Congolese soldiers.

King picked up the spent machine gun and attached a new magazine to it. Tank picked up another of the AK-47s.

"Where is the Marauder?" asked King.

"I think I saw it around back. There's a garage there," said Tank.

"Good, you and Blade go and get it and bring it around to that Administration building. I think that's where they took our gear. Salt and I will meet you there," said King.

The two teams took off together down the hallway and exited just before the interrogation room where King had been not half an hour before.

There were no more men outside. It had gone quiet. King thought for a minute, trying to count how many men had been shot by the TaXI team. Not including the Russians and the General and his Major, they had disabled five men. There would be more here, probably a platoon's worth. At least a dozen or more men. King didn't like the quietness.

He and Salt quickly made their way to the administration building. They tried the door. It was unlocked, just as he had suspected. King swung it open and faded right. Salt was right behind him and went left.

King dropped to his knee and fired a volley of bullets at two soldiers sitting at the table. Both were smoking and seemed unaware of the cacophony of sound that had not long before been erupting from the cellblock.

They were dead before they knew what hit them. On the floor on the opposite side of the dead soldiers were the bags of the TaXI team. They were open and had been rifled through. Their gear was strewn about on top of each bag, including their passports.

"Get the gear together," said King. "Make sure passports, ammo and Berettas are there."

Salt nodded and got to work. King trained his machine gun on the door which he left wide open and which gave him a great wide view of any Congolese trying to approach. Off in the distance he heard machine gun fire. It was likely Blade and Tank around back by the garage.

There sounded like an exchange of pistol fire and machine gun fire in spurts. It lasted several seconds and then everything went quiet again. All King could hear was Salt packing up the gear.

"The gear is all ready, Colonel," said Salt. "I found most of our stuff, though some small items are missing."

"The Berettas, passports, ammo?" asked King, not taking his eyes from the door.

"Nah, that's all there," said Salt. "Just some medical supplies and clothing is missing."

"Good enough," said King.

The Marauder could be heard coming around the far side of the cell block. King saw it as it turned and headed towards them with lights on.

"Let's go," said King.

He grabbed two of the duffel bags and Salt grabbed the other two. The AK-47s were slung over their shoulders when they stepped outside, as the Marauder swung around. Blade opened the backdoors and Salt and King jumped in.

"Let's finish this mission, already," said Blade.

May 8, 2012 5:53 a.m.

Minutes outside Pointe-Noire, Congo

"What's the ETA on those Tomcats coming from the USS Murdock?" asked King.

Blade looked at his tablet and tapped away at it for a moment.

"Less than three minutes, Colonel," said Blade. "And ANA is not happy about this. They said there would be no interference on our behalf."

King nodded and smiled out the window at nothing in particular.

"They aren't helping us," said King, "the US Navy is."

He was splitting hairs. The whole of the Congolese Army was practically on their tail. At least at the last count, Salt had sighted half a dozen Army trucks of assorted sizes bearing down on the Marauder.

Tank had been driving since they left Dolisie. It was getting warm as the sun was starting to bruise and then bleed all over the horizon. It was rising in the east as TaXI headed west towards Pointe-Noire, the second biggest city in Congo and where most of the Congolese oil business was located.

The USS Murdock was sitting off the coast of Angola, about one hundred kilometers west of Luanda. It was a stroke of luck. King had called in a favor from one of his old navy buddies who happened to be the Admiral in charge of the USS Murdock. Admiral Templeton Peck.

The problem was, all communication was encrypted through ANA and that's why ANA got its nose out of joint.

Salt was up in the gun turret trying to keep the Congolese at bay. He was running out of ammo.

"Colonel, I could use a little air support here, I'm running out of ammo," said Salt.

He had ducked his head in, just in time, as some stray gunfire from the lead truck ricocheted off the machine gun Salt had just moments ago been holding.

"Just a couple of minutes, Salt," said King. "Hold your horses."

Salt sighed.

"I don't have any horses left, Colonel, and two minutes is a lifetime up here."

"Well, when you run out of ammo, duck back in here and relax. Blade will fix you a nice icy beverage," said King.

Salt popped his head back up into the gun turret. The gunfire from the trucks had stopped momentarily. Maybe they were reloading. Salt checked his ammo feed. A quick look and he figured he had maybe a hundred rounds left. That was maybe a ten second burst. If he had two minutes left he could do about three seconds every thirty seconds. That might work.

Salt aimed more carefully at the front truck. This was the pest that was buzzing bullets about his face like mosquitoes. The gunner on the lead truck had just finished feeding the belt into the medium caliber machine gun. Salt sighted in and squeezed the trigger. The bullets tore up the front of the truck before making their mark on the driver.

The truck veered quickly to the right and then tumbled over on its side, cartwheeling two or three times before ending upside down on the side of the road.

That was one down, thought Salt, but he'd wasted about five seconds on that burst, trying to find his mark. The other trucks swerved to the left and then steadied out straight again. They were coming in close. Not even fifty meters behind the Marauder.

Salt figured what the hell.

"Let's go out with a bang," he said to the trucks coming up on the Marauder's backside.

They didn't hear him, but he squeezed the trigger until the bullets stopped and the trigger jammed. He watched. He had riddled the lead left truck with bullets through the radiator and taken out both tires. But he hadn't hit the driver. The gunner and the passenger, but not the driver. It didn't matter though, the driver lost control as the tires blew off the vehicle and his passenger slumped into his lap as if they were lovers. He swerved left and just like the previous truck this one toppled sideways, cartwheeling before coming to a stop.

Salt ducked into the Marauder as the trucks opened up with their machine guns. Bullets pinged and tinged against the Marauder's weary metal hide. She'd taken a lot of beatings in her short journey from Cameroon.

Salt peeked out the rear window and he didn't like what he saw.

"Colonel!" he shouted, "we need air support now," he said.

"It's coming, Salt," said King. "Keep your pants on."

"All right, we'll just sit nice and quiet, while we get cut to ribbons by those armor piercing rounds they're loading into their machine gun," said Salt, taking a seat next to Blade.

King turned around.

"Are you certain?" he asked.

Salt nodded.

"Yup, I'm surprised they hadn't used them before. Maybe they just don't have many. But Colonel, it's not gonna take many to open us up like a can of sardines," said Salt.

King nodded.

"Blade, speak to me."

Blade looked at the tablet and tapped at it for a moment.

"They're thirty seconds out," said Blade, "and they'd like some smoke."

"Salt, give them smoke, and hope to God they're gonna make it rain," said King.

Salt dug into one of the duffel bags and pulled out a flare gun. He attached a flare.

"Let them know its coming. We're pretty in pink," Salt said.

Blade tapped into the tablet. Salt popped his head out of the gun turret and fired off the flare. A beautiful pink rocket flew into the sky as the sun started leaking yellow yolk over the eastern horizon. This took the Congolese by surprise and they followed the flare's arc, losing precious time they could have used to cut open the Marauder with their armor piercing bullets.

"Tank, you're gonna have to do some magic maneuvering for the next ten or so seconds," said King.

Salt dropped back into the Marauder and took a quick look out the back.

"They're gonna open up here, Tank," he said and dropped prone to the floor with Blade.

The gunfire was the first thing they heard. Then the armor piercing rounds biting the road behind them before coming up and punching through the Marauder's shell.

Tank swerved right and then bullets cut through the right back end and exited through the left front corner of the Marauder, inches away from Tank.

Tank swerved left and the bullets cut into the Marauder through the left back end and embedded themselves into King's passenger window, one of them grazed his trapezius. The Marauder started to wobble like she was about to roll.

"I think we've lost a tire!" shouted Tank.

"Steady, T, steady" said King.

Tank wrestled with the steering wheel to gain control over the Marauder, just managing to bring it under control without it rolling over.

"Here comes the rain," said King as he looked up through the windshield at a pair of Tomcats flying towards them, just thirty or so feet off the ground.

King watched as the two Tomcats dropped a pair of air to ground missiles just as they approached the Marauder. They rocketed past the Tomcats and over the Marauder. Moments later loud explosions and fireballs erupted in a magnificent display of yellows and oranges, putting the coming sunrise to shame.

Salt got up and looked out the rear of the Marauder.

"Hell yeah!" shouted Salt, "that's a bingo."

King turned around to Blade.

"Send our friends a thank you and a note that I owe Admiral Peck a bottle of JD," said King.

There was nothing much left of the remaining four or five army trucks that had been in hot pursuit of the Marauder. Broken, charred metal and the odd tire were all that could be seen coming through the billowing charcoal gray smoke.

The Marauder limped on under the soft hands of Tank, taking the TaXI team towards the Atlantic Ocean and Pointe-Noire.

"We need to ditch this old gal," said King. "She's been good to us, but we need to get dressed into civvies and find some civilian type of transport to get us to Luanda."

"Good idea," said Tank. "I'll find us a nice rest station where we might find a decent set of wheels for the rest of the journey."

Up ahead, Pointe-Noire came into view. Being the hub of oil activity in Congo, King was hopeful that there would be plenty of gas stations dotted about. And he was right.

A Shell gas station came into view.

"That one will do, Tank," said King.

It wasn't a modern looking gas station. In fact it was decrepit. The walls needed a fresh coat of paint and the salty sea air was nibbling at the metal infrastructure like it was sugar cane.

"Park around back," said King.

Tank eased the Marauder around back of the gas station and the four of them climbed out.

"Make sure we secure it when we leave," said King to Tank. "But first I want us all in civvies."

They walked into the small station and found the washroom. They each took turns changing out of military fatigues into khaki slacks and shirts. They looked more like casual American businessmen than army soldiers.

"Okay, Tank," said King, "secure the Marauder."

Tank climbed back into the truck with his duffel bag and placed a hunk of plastic explosive, which he took out of his bag, deftly placing it on the floor in the back to the one side. On the opposite side and towards the front, he placed another hunk of plastic explosive and joined the two with one detonator.

Tank climbed out again and filled up a jerry can of gas. He came back after paying for it and soaked the insides of the Marauder as best he could with the gas. As he was finishing up, an old, blue, beat up, and rusting VW Kombi from the 60s pulled into the gas station. Its owner got out and started filling up the tank.

"Our ride has arrived," said King nodding in the direction of the VW.

"Nice choice, Colonel," said Blade. "I used to have one just like it way back when. It was my bangin' wagon. Good times."

"At least we might be able to catch some shut eye," said Salt.

"That's the plan," said King keeping his eye on the VW.

Tank came out and joined them, holding a small black box with a red switch on it.

"The Marauder is ready to be decommissioned, Colonel," said Tank.

"Good," said King. "We're gonna take that ride there."

King nodded again in the direction of the VW. The TaXI team was standing against the wall of the gas station.

The sun was making good progress, waking up from its long nightly slumber. It seemed this was one of the few gas stations open at this early hour.

The driver finished squeezing off gas into his VW. He pulled the nozzle out a couple of inches and squeezed the trigger carefully.

"How kind of him," said Blade. "He must have known we were going on a long trip."

Tank chuckled. The driver put the nozzle back and replaced his gas cap. Then he walked into the gas station. King led his men to the VW where they very quickly jumped in. Blade took the driver's seat. The keys were in the ignition.

"You've gotta love the attention to detail," he said.

"Roll," said King.

Blade turned the ignition and the old VW came to life quickly. It might have seen better days from the looks of its exterior, but the engine purred like new. Blade put it into first gear and drove off. He adjusted the rearview mirror for his height and noticed the VW's driver come running out.

"Here he comes," chuckled Blade, "and he's none to happy about it."

"Whenever you're ready," said King, "create a distraction."

"Just another twenty meters to be safe," said Tank.

The VW was gaining speed, Blade put it into third gear and the needle was coming up on forty kilometers per hour. The driver was still running fast behind them. He was yelling and cursing at them and his arms were pumping like the VW's pistons.

"Bang, bang, thanks, man," said Tank as he pushed the switch.

In the rearview mirror Blade saw the explosion a fraction of a second before he heard it. The VW buffeted and rocked gently and the driver running behind them was knocked down.

"At least nobody else will be able to get into trouble with her now," said Tank, looking fondly off at the Marauder's remains.

May 8, 2012 12:57 p.m.
Luanda, Angola

Luanda is a city of contrasts. It is both the capital of Angola and its largest city. Over one third of Angolans live in Luanda. Why? Probably for a chance of prosperity even though more than half of them live in poverty.

Driving down the dusty and dirty roads on the outskirts of the city, King saw how this poverty was stained into the very soil of this country. From the iron grip of Portugal to the now iron grip of Bembe and APLE, it was no wonder that prosperity was having a hard time raising its fragile head.

But off in the distance King saw the wealthier sects of Luanda. The districts that held Angola's upper political and business echelons as well as the foreigners who called Luanda home for short term or even longer.

TA.X.I. TO ANGOLA

The VW Kombi was cruising into Luanda in the middle of the day. As they were coming in from the outskirts of the city, the young African boys and girls who ran next to them in naked feet and frayed clothes, but with big bright smiles and hopeful hearts, started to drop off. The traffic got busier and the smog got worse.

In many areas of Luanda there was the juxtaposition of brand new, high tech construction next to a block of rundown, derelict housing. And tossed into that scrabble of new and old were the skeletal remains of buildings that had died during the Angolan war and stood like weary tombstones in the African sun. Untended and all but forgotten as Angola, led chaotically by Luanda, reached out to the ocean to exploit the oil hidden fathoms deep.

Creeping further into the twisted bowels of Luanda, four white men in a VW van didn't seem all that out of place. Luanda had its fair share of expats and foreign workers, who had come to "help" the Angolans exploit their mineral riches.

The TaXI team was tired. The six hour journey to Luanda had allowed little more than four hours of snatched sleep for each man.

They were used to this, but the lack of rest still took its toll. Salt was up driving. Not enjoying any moment of it. Traffic in this gangly metropolis of over 5 million was a frontier of winner takes all. If you were bigger, faster or braver, you went where you liked with just a cursory nod to any semblance of traffic laws.

"Find us a hotel to stay at," said King to Blade.

Blade took some time looking up hotels in Luanda.

"This place is expensive, Colonel," said Blade, "at least for anything that looks remotely decent."

"What's your idea of expensive?" asked Tank.

"Four hundred bucks a night or more seems a little pricy for a simple bedroom."

King nodded.

"Doesn't matter," he said. "If that's all they've got then that's what we'll take. Give Salt directions to the closest one."

Blade looked back down at his table.

"Ok, Epic Sana on Rua de Missao it'll be," he said.

And so they drove into the heart of the city. The beating, but congested sclerotic heart.

Reception was pleasant and the atrium was filled with white foreigners, a mixture of South African, American and European accents and tongues. The only Angolans found in here were those employed by the hotel.

An offer to carry their bags was declined by the TaXI team and they made their own way up to two adjoining suites. They all congregated around a table in the one suite. On the table was placed the tablet showing the schematic of the Presidential Palace.

"Ok," said King, "so we know from our inside informant that Bembe will be at a reception tonight. A reception for African leaders who are sympathetic to the APLE cause."

King pointed at the Presidential Palace.

"This reception starts at eight but is scheduled to go late into the night. There are going to be "comfort women" on hand for the guests and as you can imagine, many will be making use of this service. I want us to strike just after 1 a.m. when the booze has had time to take affect and the long night has tired everyone out."

"Including us," said Salt, yawning and not trying to hide it.

Tank smiled.

"That is why we're going to spend the rest of today here, sleeping. Those are orders," said King looking at his watch. The time was now 1:33 p.m.

"I can live with that," said Blade.

"Any questions?" asked King.

"What's the plan?" asked Tank. "I mean, now that things have been messed up with not having our plane here to fly Bembe right out tonight."

"I'm organizing a rental," said Blade.

"A rental?" asked Tank, raising his eyebrows.

Blade nodded.

"There is a South African ex army guy who is happy to lend planes without details. The only thing is, he's expensive, but I think we'll get a deal from him. He's also not a fan of Bembe either."

"What kind of plane does he have to lend us?" asked Salt.

Blade smiled.

"You're gonna love this," he said looking at Salt. "It's a De Havilland Otter, but he's retrofitted it to get 1,600 miles."

"Nice," said Salt, "you fucking chose that on purpose, didn't you? You know I hate boats; hell, I hate anything related to water."

Blade grinned at him and shrugged his shoulders.

"I aim to please. Just here to help you out," said Blade.

Salt nodded sarcastically. Blade tapped at the tablet on the desk and brought up mapping software.

"I figure this is a pretty good choice. We'll head out from here straight up to Accra, Ghana. That way we're not flying over Congo and Cameroon where some folks might like to shoot us down. From Accra it's an easy hop to Dakar, Senegal and from there to Casablanca, Morocco and then on to Zurich to drop off our package."

King nodded.

"Works for me," he said.

"And what if we end up killing Bembe because he won't come easy?" asked Salt.

"Always the optimist, hey?" said Tank.

"Same difference, except we're one person lighter," said Blade.

"Guys," said King, "my preference is to bring Bembe in alive. You know that, so let's keep that front and center."

May 9, 2012 12:43 a.m.

Luanda, Angola

"Okay, so we all know how this is going down," said King. "We're going to climb over the far wall, in the back corner where the light is out and the guards seldom patrol. Then we're going to scale the palace to the roof and come back around to the front side where the suites are. Salt and Tank are going down to the balcony first and will neutralize any threat. Blade and I will come in after. This is the suite that Bembe always uses."

King tapped the tablet, which showed the blueprints of the Presidential Palace.

"We'll grab him and head out. The difficult part here, is heading out the front, which we have to do. Bembe is not going to come easily so we'll have to head out the front. There'll be a firefight. Be prepared for that. Take all the ammo you can carry."

All four of them were huddled in the back of the VW Kombi around the tablet. Blade zoomed out and rotated the image to show the backside where they would scale the wall.

"The handy thing about this building is that it has old brick masonry so we should be able to climb it more easily," said Blade.

Blade rotated the image again to show the top of the roof and the line of travel that TaXI would take to the front west corner of the palace where they would then scale back down to the third floor balcony.

"Show the blueprints again," said King.

Blade pulled up the blueprints.

"This is how we'll get out," said King, tracing his finger from the bedroom down the hallway and down the two flights of stairs to the main landing. Then he trailed his finger out the main doors and onto the road.

"Easy, right?" he said.

"A walk in the park," said Salt.

They were all dressed in black cargo pants, black gloves, thin black turtlenecks under a black vest, black boots, and black ski masks. King looked at Tank.

"You've got the route to the harbor memorized?" asked King.

Tank nodded and grinned.

"I'll get us there if I have to carry you all myself," he said.

"One last look at this Bembe," said Blade, pulling up his image on the tablet.

"Remember," said King, "he'll be wearing his military dress uniform and he favors a red beret. There shouldn't be too many red berets in there."

He pointed to the palace, which loomed large off to the side of them across the road. There wasn't much activity in there; the guards at the front gate seemed drowsy if not already nodding off. Most of the lights were still on in the palace but the back corner was unlit. A floodlight had not yet been fixed.

"Okay, let's go. Let's get Bembe back to Zurich in time for Mother's Day," said King.

The four members of TaXI 3 exited the VW. Strapped across their chests were their carbines and along their outer thighs were their Berettas. Their black vests carried four extra carbine magazines and four extra Beretta 9mm hollow point magazines. King carried with him a rope and anchor and Salt had on a small black backpack.

They jogged wide, back around the palace keeping under the shadows and avoiding the street lights and the floodlights that washed the perimeter of the palace clean of scuttling cockroaches intent on trying to enter the palace grounds undetected. The problem was; that one floodlight, nobody had yet fixed.

King came up to the wall first. He threw the rope with the anchor up, which grabbed the top of the stone wall. King pulled on the rope and it held. He climbed up the ten-foot wall, followed by Blade, then Salt and Tank bringing up the rear. They lowered themselves from the top of the wall by their hands until they dropped the last three to four feet into the dark grounds.

They ran up to the wall of the palace, keeping in the shadows. King started to climb up the stone brick wall. He used a drainpipe for support, which made the going easier. Once his leg slipped out from under him, but he managed to keep his grip with his other leg and his arms.

Salt started up after King. Down at the far end of the palace grounds a guard turned the corner carrying a flashlight and AK-47.

Blade and Tank squashed themselves up against the wall. They would be difficult to see unless the flashlight caught them. The guard was coming towards them sticking to the well-trodden path. His flashlight was cutting away the darkness like a sickle. Blade and Tank would certainly be caught in its grimacing arc at some point.

Up above them, Salt slowly braced himself in the corner of two walls and reached into his backpack for his silencer. He took it out and grabbed his Beretta. He threaded the silencer onto the barrel and waited.

The light from the guard's flashlight cut Tank and Blade right in half.

"Hands up!" shouted the guard in Portuguese, coming towards them with his rifle aimed.

Salt took a breath and sighted his Beretta.

"What are you doing here?" Asked the guard.

Tank was smiling and both he and Blade had their hand's up.

"We got lost," said Blade in Portuguese, "I think we had too much to drink."

Just then the muffled sound of Salt's Beretta went off above them. Like someone beating a blanket. The guard had been hit in the chest and toppled like a spinning top to the ground.

"Shit," said Tank.

"You're welcome," said Salt, unscrewing the silencer and putting it back in his backpack.

"Hurry, gentleman," shouted King in a whisper halfway up the side of the palace. "There'll be someone coming to check on him in a minute."

Salt started back up after King, followed by Blade and Tank, once again bringing up the rear. He usually brought up the rear. No one wanted a tank falling on top of them from above.

They all scuttled up to the flat top of the palace's roof. King ran towards the front of the building, followed by the rest of them. They lined up against the short wall and peered over. Two guards were leaning against the wall below them smoking cigarettes and chatting. They seemed unconcerned, so far, about their missing comrade.

"Let's go," whispered King.

The jogged to the west side of the palace, just about one third of the way from the very front.

They peeked over the top again and below them was a large balcony. Off to their left quite a ways, on the ground, they could see the dark outline of the dead guard. He was difficult to make out in the dark.

"Confirmation?" asked King.

Salt reached into the backpack and handed the tablet to Blade. Blade took a look at the blueprints and lined them up with where they were right now.

"Confirmed, Colonel," said Blade. "Bembe should be just below us."

"Good," replied King, "let's make this quick."

Salt needed no more encouragement. He practically jumped himself over the side of the roof and started to climb down quickly. Tank followed on the other side, not as deftly as Salt but at the same speed. Salt waited a moment for Tank to reach the opposite corner of the balcony and they both jumped down softly onto the balcony. King and Blade were also halfway down.

Salt took out his infrared binoculars and looked through the French doors which were covered by closed curtains on the inside. He counted two figures and he gestured the same to Tank.

Tank nodded. Salt took out his silencer again and reattached it to his barrel. They only had the one on account of so much of their gear going up in smoke.

King and Blade were now on the balcony too. Salt and Tank went up to the French doors. Tank had his hand on the handle and Salt nodded, readying his pistol.

Tank tried the door handle slowly. It was unlocked. He pushed it down and opened the door quickly towards himself. Salt ducked into the room. There was a black man with his back towards him in a dirty white vest and red beret. His pants were around his ankles and on the bed in front of him was a blonde woman in lingerie giving him head.

She looked up and screamed. Tank came in quickly and grabbed her as Bembe turned around. Tank covered the woman's screams with his hands and told her to be quiet in Portuguese. She didn't understand so he told her again in English. She nodded, but he still held her close with his hand over her mouth.

"Keep quiet and pull up your pants slowly," said Salt in Portuguese.

Bembe nodded and slowly pulled up his pants. There was no sign of any weapons in the room after King and Blade did a quick sweep. Blade came up behind Salt and took out some plastic handcuffs.

"Put on your tunic so you look decent," said Blade.

Bembe picked up his tunic off the bed and looked at the hooker still in Tank's muscular arms. He put it on and buttoned it up.

"What do you want with me?" asked Bembe.

"Justice," said King. "You're going to be tried for warm crimes."

Bembe started to laugh then. Big belly laughs.

"Quiet," said Salt.

Bembe laughed some more, so Salt kicked him in the side of the face. Bembe started to wobble but caught his portly frame on the bed where he steadied himself. He was no longer laughing.

"You'll not get out of here alive," he snarled.

Tank finally let the woman go and he watched her closely. She didn't say anything. He put his finger to his mouth. She nodded.

King and Tank went up to the door and pressed against it.

They couldn't hear anyone outside. King looked back at Salt and Blade. Blade was cuffing Bembe.

"Okay, this is the tough part," King said. "Ready?"

Tank nodded and so did Salt and Blade. Blade un-holstered his Beretta and thrust it into Bembe's kidney, pushing him forward. The rest of the team held their carbines ready.

King opened the door and ducked out left. Tank went right. There was no one on this part of the third floor. King found it strange. Where are the guards, he thought?

King followed Tank down the hallway towards the back of the palace where the stairs were. Behind them were Blade with his arm in General Bembe's elbow and his pistol pointing carefully at his belly. They were strolling down the hallway together, Blade leading Bembe along.

Salt was bringing up the rear sweeping his rifle left and right and swiveling back behind to see if they were being followed. They made it down the hallway to the flight of stairs without incident.

The rushed down the first flight with King and Tank taking up position on the second floor as Blade, Bembe and Salt came behind them and continued down towards the first floor.

Two soldiers were seen at the far end of the hallway and they turned to look towards the back of the palace where King and Tank had their weapons pointed down the hallway towards them. The guards ducked behind some pillars, pulled up their AK-47s and let go a few rounds. They missed. King waited until the soldiers ducked out from the cover of the pillar and he fired. Bullets chews up chunks of wooden railing, bit into plaster on the pillars and met their mark on the first soldier.

King and Tank ducked back down the stairs, following Blade and Salt with Bembe between them.

On the first floor was where there was a lot of action. Most of the guests were still on this floor. The TaXI team came down the stairs landing on the west side of the main ballroom. Salt was maneuvering his carbine back and forth.

Most of the guests on this level were unarmed and political or business types.

Those who hadn't been sent into chaos by the earlier sound of gunfire now started to panic and rush for the exits as they saw the carbines and the TaXI team heading towards them.

King swept his rifle upwards towards the second floor. The second soldier ducked out from behind the pillar.

"Down!" yelled King.

Blade brought Bembe to the ground as bullets started flying around. King exchanged fire with the soldier and caught him in the legs, dropping him out of sight behind the bannister on the second floor.

"Let's go," said King.

Blade picked Bembe up. Bembe was struggling to get to his feet. Blade looked at him. The General had been hit in the belly by stray fire. His green tunic was starting to darken with red blood. Bembe stumbled forward and fell to his knees.

"Shit," said Blade. "He's been hit, Colonel."

"Will he make it?" asked King.

Blade looked Bembe over again.

"I think so, if I can get to work on him soon," said Blade.

"Here, I'll take him," said Tank. "Cover me."

Tank grabbed Bembe and tossed him over his shoulder in a fireman's lift as if he were a doll. They started for the exit. King and Salt going first, King out left and Salt out right.

Guests were still streaming by them as they exited. A couple of guards had their rifles up and pointing at the flood of people exiting. They were unsure of whether to fire or not. King and Salt weren't unsure.

They fired off some rounds and cut both the guards down. They fell to the ground. King waved Tank and Blade through. Blade was bringing up the rear now.

King and Salt flanked Tank as they made their way towards the main gates to cross the road and get into the VW again. Popcorn could be heard just behind them. Blade turned as a woman running across his path was hit by pistol fire from another guard standing just behind the main doors they had just exited. The guard fired a couple more times, missing everyone except Bembe whom he hit in the ass. Bembe wailed.

Blade brought up his pistol and double tapped him in the chest. King had spun around and noticed another soldier on the other side of the door, he was fumbling with his AK-47, which seemed to have jammed. King aimed carefully, waiting for an opportunity, as guests continued to stream past them. He fired two shots and the man fell backwards, his AK-47 lying next to him.

Tank was struggling with the fat Bembe over his shoulder, trying to jog but coming up with nothing more than a shuffle.

Tank was through the gates, with King and Salt on his sides. King was facing backwards towards the palace and Salt was facing forward. Blade had flanked just behind Salt, facing the rear as the four of them shuffled across the road towards the VW.

Guests of the Presidential Palace had started to disperse like water, left and right out the gates. King, Salt, and Blade could see no more guards at the moment as Tank made it to the VW. Salt opened the side door and Tank eased Bembe into the back. Salt climbed in and Blade came in after him. He slammed the door closed as Tank was climbing into the driver's seat.

King stood by the passenger door watching and sweeping for any sign of Angolan soldiers or security guards. The VW came to life and King quickly jumped into the passenger seat. Tank was off before King had fully closed the door.

"Shit," said Tank, "we've got company."

He saw two trucks rounding the corner from the far side of the palace, their lights bright and angry, like demons. King glanced back and saw them coming. Each truck had a machine gun on a turret and a soldier manning it.

"Salt, I need you back there," said King.

"On it, Colonel," replied Salt.

Salt bashed out the VW's rear window with the butt of his carbine and crouched down in a firing position. Blade was fumbling in his duffel bag for medical supplies, and shining a flashlight on Bembe, which he held in his mouth.

Blade took the flashlight out.

"It doesn't look good, Colonel," said Blade. "I don't know if he's going to survive the hour. There's a lot more blood than I expected. I think the bullet nicked an artery."

King turned around to look at Bembe lying on his back in the VW. Blade was kneeling over him, the flashlight on his stomach. It was wet through his clothes. The Tunic had been unbuttoned and Blade was rolling up the undershirt.

"Do your best, Blade," said King. "Try and keep him alive if you can."

Machine gun fire spluttered from the first of the army trucks about a hundred meters behind the TaXI team as Tank took a left turn, screeching around the corner, the VW lifting up on two wheels. The bullets skipped off the road and sparked against light posts.

"That's going to chew us up like confetti!" yelled Tank. "Do something, Salt."

"I'm on it, Colonel, as soon as they come around again," said Salt.

Tank was struggling to get the VW up to one hundred km/h. The roads weren't helping with their potholes. The roads were getting congested, up ahead was a traffic jam.

The army trucks turned the corner and came on strong, they were closing the gap. Salt peppered a round of carbine fire at them.

Some bullets sparked up on the front hood of the truck but didn't connect well with anything that would slow them down.

Salt turned around and reached into his duffel bag for a flashbang. Machine gun fire erupted again, this time several bullets cut into the VW, missing any human flesh by inches.

"Goddamnit, Salt, you trying to have us killed out here?" asked King.

Salt ignored the encouragement and pulled out the flashbang. He pulled the pin and threw it out the back. It bounced along the road as the army trucks came towards it. The soldiers were close enough that their yelling in Portuguese could be heard as they tried to swerve to avoid it.

"You might want to close your eyes!" yelled Salt.

Tank was slowing the VW down, looking for a side route. He pulled up onto the sidewalk and slipped right down a narrow alley. As he did, the flashbang went off.

The light from it snuck into the alley behind them, but it had lost its luminescence by then.

On the road they had just been on, the first of the army trucks drove into the back of the parked cars, the light having blinded and disoriented the driver.

The second truck was not as affected by the grenade. The driver swerved right past the crashed truck and ducked into the alley after the VW. The alley was a dirt corridor with women and men carousing along it, leaning against the walls of the buildings on either side, trying to hold them up, it seemed. Many were making out. Frightened eyes looked up at the looming van, and they ducked into little alcoves and doorways, narrowly missing being run over.

The alley was bumpy; it hadn't seen a grader in years. The army truck started firing at them again. The shots were going wild. Bullets chewed into the brick buildings on the left and the right, into the dirt behind the VW and off into the night sky like bright streamers. A couple connected with the lower backend of the VW, taking out the lights on the rear. The passenger rear tire was hit.

"Shit," said Tank, "that's gonna slow us down."

"Steady, Tank, we've only got another click or two left to go," said King.

Salt grabbed a grenade from his bag. He pulled the pin and tossed it out the back. It bounced a couple of times on the dusty alley and stopped several meters in front of the oncoming truck. The driver saw it and slammed on the breaks. That was an error, he should have rather tried to accelerate past it before it exploded, which he might have been successful doing.

Instead, the tires slid over the dirt and the gunner flew over his turret landing awkwardly on the dirt just ahead of the grenade. The grenade blew up crippling the truck and killing the gunner were he lay.

"The threat has been eradicated, Colonel," said Salt, sliding in towards the middle of the van to see if he could give Blade a hand.

Blade was trying to plug the bullet opening in Bembe's stomach with a salve that was cauterizing the wound. He was having modest success.

"I really need a clinic to help him," said Blade.

King turned around to look at Blade.

"It is ANA's preference to have him brought in alive, but it is not a requirement. Just do what you can," said King.

TA.X.I. TO ANGOLA

May 9, 2012 1:27 a.m.

Luanda harbor, Angola

Johannes VanRensburg was waiting patiently for TaXI to arrive. The scheduled time was for 1:30 a.m. He was standing on one of the small jetties that jutted off the main harbor that was of a better height for accessing the small De Havilland Otter. He was smoking a cigarette. The lit end burning red like a twinkling light.

This part of the harbor was quiet. Off a ways, there was activity on the docks with men lifting large transport containers off a ship that had just recently docked while VanRensburg had watched.

He was getting out of Angola. The place was going to the dogs, especially ever since Bembe and his APLE movement had started terrorizing everyone in the major cities.

The small rural villages didn't count. There wasn't much of a resistance movement, not when there wasn't much international light being shed on the sad plight of the Angolans. A people he had come to love and admire in the twenty years he had spent here.

From a distance, you might mistake Johannes for Indiana Jones. He wore the same style fedora, khaki pants and leather vest. What he didn't have was a whip. He preferred, instead, a pistol. A 9 mm Vektor SP1.

Johannes flicked his cigarette away as he saw the VW's lights sweeping across the distance as Tank turned the VW towards the harbor. It wasn't going fast. It was down to three good wheels and that was slowing them down.

Johannes jumped into the cockpit and started up the plane. The propeller spun around slowly two times and then jerked to life. He adjusted the throttle and let it idle as he waited. Johannes wondered why they hadn't asked for much gear for their long flight to Senegal.

He had been told that these American soldiers of fortune wanted the plane as light as possible with as much fuel as possible.

He had been happy to oblige, especially once the ten thousand dollars had been wired to his account in South Africa.

Ten thousand dollars for just a three-day rental was a great deal for him. This plane had been sitting empty for several weeks. Costing him money.

As the VW came up to the harbor, Johannes walked up to greet them and help them. King jumped out of the passenger side and opened up the side door for Salt and Blade. Under the dim harbor lights Johannes could see the holes in the side of the van and the blown out tire.

"You guys took a beating, hey?" he said in his thick South African accent.

King turned around and grinned at him.

"We've taken worse," he said.

Blade leaned into the van and helped ease Bembe out of the back. He grabbed his wrist and put Bembe's arm around his shoulder. Bembe slumped up against Blade, feeble and wobbly on his feet. His face was cast downward and his mouth drooled, pink, bubbly gobs of spit. His breathing was labored and shallow. His eyes fluttered and remained mostly closed.

Johannes looked at Bembe and took his chin in his hand and lifted his face towards the light. Johannes shook his head.

"This is not General Bernardo Bembe," said VanRensburg.

King looked up at him. Blade looked at him too. They both frowned. Salt cursed under his breath. Bembe managed a smirk.

"Are you sure?" asked King, "he looks like him."

Johannes nodded.

"Bembe has a large mole on the backside of his left ear, here," Johannes said, folding the impostor's ear forward revealing no mole.

"Also," said Johannes, "Bembe has a nasty burn on his left shoulder."

King took rolled up the impostor's sleeve to reveal a smooth, unblemished shoulder.

"Shit," he said.

"So who is this?" he asked to himself.

"Bembe's doppelganger," offered Blade.

"So where the hell is the real Bembe?" asked Salt.

"You will not find him," said the impostor, the first words out of his mouth.

Salt whipped out his Beretta and put a bullet in the back of the man's head. He went limp in Blade's arms before Blade realized what had happened and let him go.

"Jesus, Salt," said Blade. "I'm standing here."

King looked at Salt with a cold stare and slowly shook his head.

"I told you to behave," said King. "Never again."

Salt holstered his pistol and looked down at the ground.

"Never again, you understand?" asked King, in barely a whisper. "You don't take out our package without my say so, first."

Salt nodded.

"Sorry, Colonel, he was a dead man walking anyway, right Blade?" said Salt.

Blade didn't say anything.

"You drag him into the harbor now, by yourself," said King.

Salt grabbed the impostor's legs and dragged him off to the edge of the jetty where he then rolled him into the ocean.

King turned to Tank and Blade.

"The Russians must have gotten here first to inform them," said King.

Johannes nodded.

"It's going to be harder for you guys now," he said.

"Not if they think we've left with Bembe," said Tank.

King nodded. Johannes did too.

"That's a good idea," said Johannes. "I don't think these guys know you're with me. And you weren't followed right?"

Blade nodded.

"No, we lost them a ways back," he said.

"Good," said Johannes, "then you can come and stay with me until the dust has settled before you go for the real Bembe."

May 11, 2012 9:09 a.m.
Luanda, Angola

Johannes VanRensburg lived on the outskirts of Luanda, about forty kilometers out, in a trailer that was exceedingly small for the four TaXI members and him. But it was far enough out of the way that nobody really paid any attention to this white South African living on the fringes of Angolan society and trying to rent his planes.

Johannes had gone into the harbor on the tenth to see if any of the oil companies could use some of his planes. He was keeping everything the same as it had been. From all accounts nobody had suspected that the TaXI team was still around. Johannes' informants assured him that the APLE leaders felt even more confident that they had pulled one over on the Americans hell bent on destabilizing their plans.

King looked out of the small trailer on a wide expanse of land. It was dusty outside. Unlike much of the rest of Africa they had a chance to safari through to get here, Angola was much drier. This part they were in was particularly drier. Known as Miradouro da Lua or the Watchpoint of the Moon. In fact, looking out the dirty and dusty window King felt like he might not be far from some areas of the Grand Canyon.

A decade or so feet away from the trailer was an old Datsun 720 crew cab they had borrowed from the harbor. It had a truck cap on the back for them to store their gear. Tonight was hopefully going to be the night they were going to finish this tour.

At the front end of the trailer, King could hear and smell the sizzling of Johannes cooking bacon and probably eggs.

Johannes came down the trailer and put his hand on King's shoulder.

"Breakfast is ready," he said.

King nodded, still staring out the window.

"You'll get your guy," said Johannes.

"Alive, I hope," answered King.

Johannes went back to the kitchen and slid piles of bacon rashers onto five plates. He also put two eggs on each plate and brought them out to the small table in the middle of the trailer. He went back to the kitchen and brought out a plate piled high with ten slices of toast.

Salt and Tank were already sitting. Both of them were salivating and eyeing their plates. Blade came out of the toilet and King and he sat down across from Salt and Tank. Johannes sat at the one end of the table closest to the kitchen. He put his hands together and closed his eyes and prayed.

TaXI waited patiently for him to finish. Salt swallowed, still looking at the two buggy yellow eyes of his eggs. Amens were voiced around the table after Johannes had finished. King was pleased that Johannes had put in a good word to the man above for TaXI to get Bembe for good this time. Something about God's hand striking fear in their enemies.

Not that Johannes knew about TaXI. These were just mercenaries. But still, as long as they were out to get Bembe, Johannes was on their side.

Blade grabbed two slices of toast and slathered them with margarine and marmalade.

Everyone else in turn took their two slices of bread and started digging in. King buttered his toast with the margarine and lay bacon across it in a very orderly fashion. He topped each slice of toast with an egg and then slit the egg's eye and smeared the yellow yolk all over the bread. These were over easy.

Johannes finished first and looked over at Blade's plate. The bacon and eggs were undisturbed.

"You don't like my cooking," he said with a smile.

Blade smiled back.

"No, I'm vegetarian," said Blade.

"Why didn't you say so," said Johannes. "What about the eggs though?"

"No eggs or dairy either."

"Okay, let me get you some more toast."

Johannes got up and went back into kitchen to make more toast. Salt eyed Blade's plate. Blade pushed it forward.

"It's a buffet," he said. "You guys help yourself."

They didn't need encouraging. Like vultures around a fresh kill, the plate was picked clean within seconds. Johannes came back with four more slices of toast, a banana and an orange.

"This is all I've got, sorry," he said.

"That's plenty, thanks," said Blade.

After breakfast and after Johannes had driven off into the city again, King called a meeting. The four of them sat around the same breakfast table, which was now empty.

"So, we know from our informant that Bembe is scheduled to depart the airport tonight at 11:00 p.m. for Lubango to quell a small uprising there instigated by some farmers. This is when I want us to grab him," said King.

Blade had the tablet on the table and tapped at it, bringing up the airport in Luanda.

"On the northwest side of the airport is a hangar, where we have been told, Bembe's Fokker 50 will be ready and waiting for his flight to Lubango," continued King.

"I can fly that," said Blade.

King nodded.

"That is the plan," said King. "We want to get there before Bembe and his clan arrive, secure the plane and defeat any threat before we grab him and bring him onboard for a pampered flight to Geneva."

"What time is Bembe scheduled to depart?" asked Tank.

"Our man on the inside tells us his flight is scheduled for 11:11 p.m., for some numerological reason I don't quite understand. The thing is," said King, "he's going to have a security squad with him. Probably his top six to ten guys. It would be more, but because he thinks we've gone, he's just going with his regular outfit."

"Thank God we're not flying a boat anymore," said Salt.

Blade smiled and elbowed him.

"I'll make sure to make it as bumpy as possible," he said.

Salt shrugged.

"So, I want us there at the hangar and in position by 10 p.m. Bembe's known for his fastidiousness and timeliness," continued King.

Blade had his arms folded in front of his chest.

"The one problem I see is that the Fokker, love that name, only has a range of around two thousand clicks. We need a range of around twenty five hundred clicks if we're going to do our Luanda to Accra to Dakar to Casablanca to Geneva hops," said Blade.

King smiled.

"I thought we'd just try and wing it, see how it goes. But seriously, our informant has said that this Fokker is actually outfitted with an additional fuel tank, giving it close to that twenty-five hundred range you want. Thing is, we're going to have to make sure it is fueled fully because it isn't likely to be for the short trip to Lubango," said King.

"So we're just gonna hijack a fuel truck when we're at the airport and fill 'er up, Colonel?" asked Tank not quite believing.

"Yes, you are," replied King.

"Me," said Tank pointing his finger to his chest.

King nodded.

"I have all the faith in you," he said.

"I like it," said Salt. "Let's get this shit show over and done with."

TA.X.I. TO ANGOLA

May 11, 2012 9:49 p.m.

Quatro de Fevereiro International Airport, Luanda, Angola

The evening was warm and sweaty. Tank was out of the Datsun and cutting open the chain link fence on the southwest side of the airport. A plane was coming in to land on the long landing strip. It was an Air France Boeing.

The international airport in Luanda was now in the heart of the city; shanty houses and other buildings straggled along its perimeter. The section they were in was the only sparsely populated area around the airport. It was dusty and clumped with vegetation, and small bushes dwarfed by lack of consistent water.

The night sky was dark and Tank was working by the light of the stars and moon. Additional yellow haze spilled towards him from the lights from the airport and landing strip. It wasn't much; they were mostly in the comfortable embrace of darkness.

TA.X.I. TO ANGOLA

There were a few buildings scattered randomly in this unpopulated area of the airport's land and none of them had any lights on. Tank snipped away at the chain, the crunch and soft twang of each cut wire marking a slow rhythm.

Salt was in the back along with Blade. Their bags were in the back under the truck cap with easy access thanks to Salt having broken out the back window. They were fully prepared.

They had lots of ammo still and several grenades and flashbangs left. Salt licked his lips. He was eager to get this done with.

He was upset and indignant that they had been fooled on the first attempt. He would make sure that didn't happen again.

King was in the front passenger seat chewing on a small piece of sugarcane he had taken from Johannes' trailer. He was watching Tank and scanning the rest of the airport for any problems.

They were all dressed in their finest black paramilitary gear. They weren't over dressed, but they were still hot. It was twenty-seven degrees Celsius. Uncomfortably warm, and the damp air was humid and wet, like dog's breath.

King was plotting the course to the hangar. They'd have to drive northeast along the landing strip for almost two kilometers. Then they'd tack north for a couple hundred meters and then jog northeast again for just over half a kilometer, and then meander behind a gaggle of grounded aircraft for cover. From there, they'd cross the last one hundred meters by foot.

The problem was with the first eighty percent of the trip. There was too much driving parallel to the runway for King's liking. They would be easier to see with the lights dotted like flares along the landing strip for King to feel fully secure.

The saving grace was that at this time of night on Friday evening there wasn't a lot of activity.

They had been here coming on five minutes and the only plane he'd seen was the one that had just passed.

Tank finished cutting open the wire fence. He rolled it back wide enough for the Datsun to fit in and tied it off top and bottom with zip ties. He climbed back into the driver's seat, passing the bolt cutters back, where Blade took them from him.

It wasn't dark enough for night vision, and with the runway lights it would be easy going. The Datsun's engine was idling softly like a purring kitten. The lights were off.

"Okay, everybody know what they're doing?" asked King.

Everybody murmured in agreement.

"Let's go, then," said King.

Tank put the truck into first gear and rolled on through the open fence. It caught the side of the truck, screeching as if it was in pain.

"Oops," said Tank.

"Oops is right," said Blade.

"Guess I didn't cut it wide enough," said Tank.

"You think?" said Salt. "You're gonna wake up the whole of Luanda like that."

"It's not that bad," said Tank, looking at Salt from the rearview mirror.

And then they were through the hole and driving parallel to the runway in the ditch. Staying low was keeping the minimum of light on them. They made quick work of the first part and coming up across the runway, Tank stopped to see if there was any traffic coming, from above or at ground level.

The airport was quiet. The road joining the two runways was empty and Tank eased up over the long runway and got onto the road, which had no lights along its side.

Tank slipped off the tarmac as soon as he could, heading north on a small dusty road, staying close to the corrugated building of a private air company that was closed for the night.

Tank made his way across the shorter runway and kept low, under the wings of planes parked haphazardly across from the runway. He pulled up under the wing of an Airbus 320 that was whitewashed and held no insignia of any airline. He put the truck into first gear, engaged the handbrake and turned off the ignition.

King looked around; there were some lights on inside the hangar. The main hangar door was open and the nose of the Fokker was pointing out. He looked at the time on his watch and it read 9:57 p.m.

Salt was looking to his left and then right. Just to the left of the hangar was a fuel truck. It was running and its lights were flooding the tarmac in front of it.

"Okay, here we go," said King. "Stay low, bring your bags and we'll enter on the left side. Salt you'll come with us until we've neutralized any threats. Then you can go and grab that fuel tank."

"Sure, Colonel," said Salt.

"And listen," continued King, "we don't want to damage that plane, so if you're gonna fire, fire at close range and use single shot trigger."

King opened the door and climbed out. The others exited after him, closing the doors quietly. Salt came around to the back of the truck and opened the cap. He pulled out the four duffel bags and each man took his own. Then Salt pulled out the carbines. They strapped them over their chests. Their Berettas were already attached to the thigh in their holsters.

King lead them in a crouch, zig zagging under the wings of the last few planes before darting across the tarmac and over to the southwest side of the hangar. He kept low and wide of the front floodlights that poured their light liberally over the front of the hangar.

King noticed two men in blue uniforms in the hangar. Most likely mechanics or janitors. There were two other men at the back of the hangar in military fatigues and carrying AK-47s.

Salt came up and lined up against the metal side of the hangar behind King. He was followed by Blade and then Tank bringing up the rear. King gave notice with his hand to enter the hangar.

King went first and peeled left as he entered around the left side of the open hangar door. Salt followed him, peeling left as well and staying back and slightly to the right of King. Blade slipped in and veered off right, across the nose of the plane, followed by Tank who stayed slightly behind him and to his left.

The two men in blue uniforms looked up. The one man was holding a clipboard, which he dropped in fright.

"Down on the ground!" yelled King in Portuguese.

The mechanics dropped like puppets whose strings had been cut. They lay face first on the cool concrete floor of the hangar.

The soldiers pulled their AK-47s up and towards the intruders, but they were too slow. Salt let off two shots, hitting the one soldier twice in the chest. He dropped like a heavy load of laundry. Blade squeezed off three rounds at the soldier stationed on his side. All three met their mark and the man was dead before he hit the ground.

Salt and Tank kept cover while King and Blade tied the two mechanics with zip ties and then dragged them into the back of the hangar where a small office was located. They pushed them into the office and tied them back to back to each other. They also secured their legs and gagged them. King told them if they made a noise, they'd be killed. The men nodded, their eyes wet and scared.

King and Blade came back out of the office.

"Take a look at the cockpit and familiarize yourself with the plane. Fire it up, too, just so we're sure it's gonna fly," said King.

Blade nodded and climbed up the stairs into the fuselage and then entered the cabin.

Salt and Tank were stationed on either side of the open doorway, scanning for any unwanted attention. King walked up to Tank.

"I'd like us to use the element of surprise," he said to Tank. "All four of us will hide behind a tanker as soon as Salt has fueled up the plane. I'll have him bring it just off to the side at an angle so that we have line of sight, but enough room to get the plane out."

Tank nodded and King went over to speak with Salt.

"Go get the fuel tanker and fill up the Fokker. Hopefully, you'll empty it and then we can use it as cover, parking it just over there," said King pointing out to his left just off from the hangar. "That will give us line of sight and protection. I want Bembe and his men to enter the hangar before we flashbang them and start the firefight before they have a chance to realize what has even gone on."

Salt nodded and exited the hangar to locate the fuel tanker. King and Blade stood guard. It was now 10:11 p.m.

TA.X.I. TO ANGOLA

May 11, 2012 11:01 p.m.

Quatro de Fevereiro International Airport, Luanda, Angola

Blade was squished in tight between Salt and Tank. Thank heavens everyone had bathed that morning and used deodorant. The TaXI team was crammed into a small metal shed just in front of and attached to the right side of the hangar as you approached it. A few rivets had been popped out and King and Salt were looking through them watching for Bembe and his men. The tanker had too much fuel left in it to use as cover and on second thoughts it was going to look way out of place out there on the tarmac. They didn't need to cause any suspicion.

"Here they come," whispered Salt.

Blade leaned forward, as did Tank, to see out the tiny holes in the shed.

TA.X.I. TO ANGOLA

A black, older model, Mercedes sedan pulled up, followed by a green army truck. A soldier dressed in tunic and pants, opened the rear door and got out. He went around the back of the car and opened up the opposite door. Bembe climbed out and stood for a moment looking around. His underling closed the door behind him and tapped the roof. The Mercedes drove off.

In the green truck, six soldiers jumped out the back and formed a circle around Bembe and his underling. These men were armed with machine guns and side arms. They opened up the circle as Bembe strode through them and started for the hangar. To his left was the man who had opened his door. Behind them, the six security officers followed, casually, arrogantly, without concern for their safety.

As they entered the hangar, King gestured for his team to exit the shed. Salt pulled the pins on both flashbangs. King opened the door as quickly and quietly as possible. It creaked.

They rushed to the hangar's opening just as the Angolans were turning around to identify the sound. Salt lobbed in the two flash bangs and the TaXI team ducked out and just behind the open door. Three seconds later the flashbangs went off.

Salt rushed in followed by King, Blade and Tank. The Angolans were dazed and confused, shouting, groaning and looking around, trying to regain their sight.

Salt shot three of the security contingent before they knew what had hit them. Blade came up behind one and shot him in the heart. Tank shot two rounds into a fifth and King took out Bembe's underling and the last of the security soldiers.

King reached out for Bembe and brought him to the ground.

"You're coming with us, General," said King.

Blade came up and cuffed Bembe with metal handcuffs. He pulled him up and looked at the fat man. He folded his left ear down and identified Bembe's mole. They had the real Bembe this time. Bembe was grimacing and gritting his teeth.

"Who are you?" he asked in Portuguese.

"Your worst nightmare," said King. "General Bernardo Bembe, you're wanted for crimes against humanity. You will be tried by the International Court of Justice in The Hague, after you've been formerly arrested by the All Nation's Alliance in Zurich."

Bembe tried to smile as broadly as he could.

"What about my phone call?" he asked.

"This isn't the States, funny boy," said Blade.

King nodded at Blade and he walked Bembe up into the airplane. Salt and Tank went around prodding the seven men that now lay like sleeping babies, weeping blood. They pulled them off to the side and then climbed up into the plane as the propellers started.

"Good job, men," said King. "Another good pay day for us and we'll likely get this menace to Zurich in time for Mother's Day. A bonus for that."

Salt smiled. Tank looked over at Bembe, and he looked like a man defeated. Bembe's head was hanging low. Tank closed his eyes and felt thankful. Thankful that another African despot was finally seeing justice.

ABOUT JASON BLACKER

Jason Blacker was born in Cape Town but spent most of his first 18 years in Johannesburg. When not grinding his fingers down to stubs at the keyboard he enjoys drinking tea, calisthenics and running. Currently he lives in Canada.

Under his own name he writes hard boiled as well as cozy mysteries, action adventure, thrillers, literary fiction and anything else that tickles his muse. Jason Blacker also writes poetry and daily haikus at his haiku blog.

You can find his haikus and other poetry at his website **www.haiqueue.com**.

To stay up to date and learn about new releases be sure to visit **www.jasonblacker.com** where you can find more information about his writing and upcoming projects.

If you enjoy space opera in the tradition of Star Trek then take a look at Jason Blacker's pen name "Sylynt Storme". It is under the name **Sylynt Storme** where you can find both sci-fi and vampire fiction written by Jason Blacker.

"Star Sails" is the space opera series and **"The Misgivings of the Vampire Lucius Lafayette"** is his vampire series.